CW00857997

Prologue - *PRESENT DAY*

Sitting by the fire, the flames crackling joyfully, he found his thoughts drifting back again to when the heat of a fire meant death, destruction and chaos. He tried to close his mind to the events that he had witnessed and been a part of. He longed for peace and pure rest, the kind that only a simple death can bring.

The kind he knew he could never have. The world of 2050 repeatedly knocked at his door, yet he had no desire to let it in.

No-one beyond himself knew the truth behind the medals and tales of heroism, though it hovered like a vulture in the dark waiting for the last breath of reason to issue forth.

Now, he had the need to put everything into perspective, to clarify in his own mind exactly what he had been through, to admit to the horrendous things he had found himself capable of doing. Yet he could not write down a word nor even a syllable, for the battle still raged within him. Much as he might not wish it, he was still a key player, searching for hope amongst the confusion that now reigned on Earth.

He had not witnessed all that he knew, first hand. He knew many more things simply through the connection that held everyone together. Yes, he had learned much from others. There seemed to be no gaps in his wisdom, he knew the lives of many different people and could build truth from the feelings of others, which flowed through him. For this story, he was all seeing, all knowing.

It seemed to begin in the year 2022 by a meteor that passed close to the Earth, the internet was destroyed, mobile phones no longer worked. A plague wiped out most people over fifty and many over forty years old. By 2023 the world had become desperate. Each country had closed its borders trying to prevent the inevitable from happening. The infection was in the very marrow of the planet's structure.

Menarty picked up his pen and started to write but the words wouldn't come. He sunk back into the easy chair by the fire and watched it flicker until he drifted into an uneasy sleep, his hand resting on a small silver revolver.

Chapter 1

Alex Cartier had been almost twenty-four, and lived an amiable life, socializing with the rich and powerful in England, before it became the first casualty in a world war that was to be fought by creatures from other worlds.

He had been attending a party at the Ritz hotel in London. The economic climate in Britain was harsh with little sign of any political party knowing how to avoid a new depression. Something in the food chain, during the previous few years, had caused billions of people to die, more was now expected of the young. They found themselves in high powered or dangerous jobs with little or no training. However, this New Year was the best ever for Alex. He had just been promoted at his bank. His childhood spent watching thrillers, action and Bond films had spurred him to allow MI5 to recruit him. His cover, which was that of a banker had been easily arranged by his grandfather before he died, his future looked bright and all seemed well with his world.

He was tall, dark haired and classically handsome. So far everything in his life had gone the way he had wanted it to. He was lucky to have been trained by the secret service in martial arts, marksmanship, survival skills, German, Japanese and Russian and many things that he never thought he would have a use for, but that were fun to learn anyway.

He had never known his parents. They had been killed in a motoring accident when he was two. Because of this, his rich grandfather had indulged his every whim. Sometimes Alex suspected that he never really would rise above what he thought of as his "cover" as a banker.

His dreams of saving the world from some mad scientist or rescuing a beautiful girl from certain death had long evaporated and his banking career seemed far more worthwhile.

His upbringing had been highly privileged, private schools, somewhat overprotected perhaps, nothing had ever been expected from him. Goals had

3

always been set very low, then suddenly the population of the world dwindled dramatically and he knew much more would now be asked of him. His grandfather had died only a few months ago and Alex still felt his loss. The millions he had inherited had done nothing to get rid of the pain.

He had arrived at the Ritz, for the party, with a beautiful woman called Cassandra. Many of the big names in banking were there and as usual he circulated with his girlfriend, like a prize, hanging on his arm. She had long flowing red hair and a pert nose that made her face particularly pretty. Alex would be talking to someone and then catch her looking wistfully off into the night and his own thoughts would drift to later when they would be alone. She was a few years older than him and he looked forward to the end of the party when he could take her home and they would drink champagne and make love by a roaring fire. Alex was nothing, if not romantic. The plague had wiped out so many people but the loss of the electronic devices, phones and the internet had made the loss seem less. Countries no longer communicated in the same way and the news was brief and to the point.

They had been together for three months and he envisaged many more. He winked at her across the ballroom and was rewarded with a dazzling smile. She hated these banking industry parties but put up with them for his sake. She found him witty and charming and was looking forward to spending a couple more months with him before looking for "mister right". He was a handsome man, but she did not think that he had that edge she so admired in other men, the kind of men who could stand up for themselves – and her, too, for that matter – and fight if need be. She glanced at her watch, he had promised that they could leave just after midnight, it was just half eleven.

Alex was talking to an old man with a short white beard, though he was not really listening. His attention was alerted to someone on his left moving through the party. He was unlike anyone else in the room, though he was dressed in evening clothes, an unnatural aura surrounded him driving the air from the room as he walked by. There was nothing in particular, his clothes looked right, except they were not quite pressed enough and although his hair looked combed, it was also out of place and foreign to his body. Indeed it was his movement that was so strange, as if walking had become an unmanageable feat, as though his joints did not quite fit in their sockets and were getting more out of alignment as he moved. Alex watched as other members of the party also turned towards the intruder that now, like a toy being manoeuvred by an amateur puppeteer. It made its way jerkily across the room and sat heavily down on a hard backed chair, admitting a large belch as he did so.

The host was already making his way over and although they tried to avert their eyes, too many of the guests were consumed with morbid curiosity and disgusted humour, unable to look away.

The strange man had yellow spittle running down the side of his mouth, he looked blankly at the wealthy banker towering above him. Alex found he could see far more detail than he wanted and glanced uneasily at Cassandra moving quickly to her side.

Sub-consciously he took her by the elbow and began to glide her away. Two security men passed them. Alex glanced back. It was as if a shadow had fallen across his face, his spine tingled as a shiver raced up it and froze him with a feeling of dread and something worse, as if he had found his fate and the face of it was terrifying.

The man in the chair seemed to know the security men were bearing down on him before they reached him. His eyes had been closed ignoring the host's recriminations when suddenly his eyelids flew open, wider than should be possible, to reveal black demon-like pits. Alex had moved back towards him almost unknowingly, needing to see what was going on, as if his future depended on it.

The soul-less eyes looked down at its clenched hand, it unrolled to produce long fingers with six inch nails on them. It reached up with a sudden movement and sent the index finger, now a sharp talon straight up the nose of the host, standing as he did so, lifting him off the ground. He appeared a lot taller than when he had wandered in, as if his body was stretching and growing. They all heard the sound of tearing flesh as it pierced and pushed into the host's brain. He started to convulse as his feet dangled a few centimetres above the ground where the thing had lifted him.

The security men stopped in their tracks. Their mouths were wide open as they gaped at the monstrosity before them. They were not armed and unsure of their next move, everyone seemed frozen. The creature seemed to breathe something in and then lowered the lifeless body onto its feet. It removed its long jagged finger with a slight mushing sound and the dead man slumped to the ground, blood seeped from his nose.

The room emptied pretty quickly at that point. People just broke from their stupor and made for the exit. Alex was pushed along with the tide of screaming people. Cassandra was ahead of him, already in the hotel lobby. Behind, Alex could hear shouting and furniture breaking, than a body flew through the air and knocked a group of five including Alex, to the floor. He fell near the wall, not too far from the front desk. A telephone kiosk was nearby and one of the guests was on the phone.

"It's not human anymore! Send the team... it's just killed someone. There are dead people here... The Ritz hotel, hurry. Make sure the men are heavily armed... Make sure."

The man suddenly let go of the phone and dropped down on to the floor where Alex was still winded. He looked around to see what had struck them and saw the headless body of John Sutton, the host.

He started to get to his feet as the others did.

"No," the man hissed, "don't move, it will sense you. We just have to wait for help to arrive. You must do exactly as I say; I know what we are dealing with, my name is Raymond Courtney. You must trust me." The man spoke very calmly.

Something in his voice made Alex take note; he sank back to the floor but several other people who had heard still tried to run.

Cassandra had been carried away by the vast majority of people into the cold safe drizzle of the street. The hotel desk clerk rushed towards them wringing his hands, he tried to help people up. He was facing Alex, talking to him but Alex couldn't hear him over a wailing sound that filled the air. The clerk's face went a bright shade of white, brilliant enough for a paint

6

commercial and Alex knew the monster was now in the lobby. The man in the phone booth sank further to the ground, he tried to make himself flat and seemed to be holding his breath. The clerk ran and hid behind his counter while the men on the floor started crawling towards the revolving doors, cool air and life. Alex wanted to join them, but Courtney indicated for him to stay still and a new part of Alex listened to him. A great urge to turn round and see how far the creature was from him was gaining momentum in Alex's head, yet he resisted.

Raymond Courtney's eyes were transfixed on something behind Alex. The desk clerk was now crying behind the counter, his muffled sounds could easily be heard across the lobby where Alex and Courtney were. Something moved behind Alex and brushed his elbow, he dare not turn. Two men made a run for the door as if safety was merely getting out of the hotel.

The thing behind Alex moved past him. He would see it soon and it would see him. He kept telling himself he had to move to live but he couldn't. It passed within a couple of feet dragging some poor unfortunate person by their nostrils, it now had two talon like fingers wedged in their face. It brushed Alex's shoulder with the body, stopped and then looked directly at him, it was less than a foot away. The eyes were completely black and from the way its head moved Alex was sure that it was now blind. It couldn't see him but it knew he was there.

The face was terribly contorted, its legs appeared broken and moved both ways as though double jointed. The yellow spittle had increased to a large dribble mingled with red and grey particles. The eyes were more lifeless than a dead salmon and far more bulging.

The men had reached the outside and rolled into salvation until the thing dropped its current prey and leapt after them on all fours, its spine curved and forced its way through its now ludicrous evening dress. It grabbed them both from the street as they reached out to their loved ones and threw them back into the hotel. In a manic frenzy it slapped their heads together and threw them in the air only to spring on top of them when they landed.

Alex thought he was going to pass out with the fear and revulsion.

"Quick! move here!" Courtney was speaking from the telephone box again.

Alex wanted to move but was afraid to. "I can't" he said as softly as he could. Yet the sound of his own voice sent icicle fingers around his body. He looked over to the creature which feasted on its prey the dead eyes looking off into space and wondered if it had heard.

"Move to me" Courtney said again "when it returns to the body, near you, it will hear you."

Alex did not move at first, he had seen what happened to those who tried to get away. But now he was facing it, he could see what it was doing and it was just too awful to watch. His breathing was erratic, as the blood pumped through his body he was sure that the creature would pounce on him at any moment.

"Move slowly, it won't see you if you move slowly," Courtney sounded desperate.

With a great effort Alex crawled over to the telephone booths, he kept his line of sight on Courtney's face and tried to ignore the images he could see from the corner of his eyes. He reached Courtney at the telephone kiosk while the monster was still eating his appetizer.

Suddenly the creature rushed over to where Alex had been a few moments earlier and reclaimed the body he had been dragging. He sniffed in the air and moved his long arms around. When it stopped moving, it looked straight at the two men by the telephones. Alex's heart began to beat so fast and loud that he thought he would surely die of fear before it got to him.

It was about to come for them when two policemen arrived in the building. They were not armed.

The monster swivelled its neck without turning around and turned its attention to the men in blue, its razor like fingers gesticulating in a strange trance like way. Its fingers were all over six inches long now and Alex wondered obscurely how it had found evening gloves that fit. His mind was trying to shut down, the part of him that had been Alex Cartier was about to be extinguished forever but something had awakened within him that was prepared to fight for survival.

"Hell Jim, this is some freak. You had better call for back up," one policeman said to the other.

"Could you come towards us please sirs?" Jim said in a calm voice.

Alex suddenly realized that the officer was talking to Courtney and himself. He looked to his new companion to see what they should do. Courtney's face was firmly turned away from them and Alex knew why, he barely dared to breathe as he looked back to the officers.

The boy behind the desk gave a sigh and slumped to the floor. The movement was not lost on the creature, it leapt like a cat it, behind the counter. It took hold of the boy before the body hit the floor.

"Leave that man alone sir and calm down please, you've had too much…" His voice trailed away as he took in the full scene "…blood" he said finally. The other policeman rushed in and tried to grab the thing before it smashed the boys head against the wall hard enough for the skull to crack like a coconut. It lashed out with its strange leg kicking the officer away, clear across the lobby to our phone area. Alex stayed where he was, not through cowardice but because he knew it would kill him if he moved. Courtney, however, had gone over to the policeman who had been thrown across the lobby. The man was still alive and Alex's new friend was trying to pull him over to the telephone area. This did not seem like such a good idea to Alex; to put all of its food in one place. The kiosk area had started to feel like a larder.

Jim suddenly turned tale and ran, presumable to call out the armed police, this thing needed to be shot and shot and shot. Words kept ringing in Alex's ears, just shoot it a couple of hundred times. If only he carried a gun, if only they had not come this evening, if only...

It had cracked open the boy's head and had started to eat. Alex couldn't see this from where he was, but he had seen it already, now he was being treated to just the sound, scraping, chewing and sucking. An eternity seemed to pass, though probably a few seconds. It belched and stood up. It seemed even taller now, the legs were somehow longer, its face had taken on a more pointed goblin type of look. It looked much thinner too, more muscled but less flab as though it had been working out during dinner.

Lightly it sprang over the counter and leapt across the lobby almost landing on Alex, he bit his tongue to stop the scream from coming out and looked towards his friend, and the policeman, who was gaining consciousness.

The creature wandered aimlessly about the lobby searching for the policeman it knew to be here somewhere. It was getting nearer to Courtney who held his hand over the mouth of the cop. A few more steps and it would be on them. Alex wondered how he could just lie there and do nothing while it killed another human being and then he realized that he couldn't listen to it eat again.

A pen lay on the floor beside him; he picked it up slowly without making any sound and then threw it far over to his right, the opposite direction to the front door. The moment the pen landed the creature was upon it in one leap, almost seeming to fly. Those strange legs that had been reforming themselves now resembled the back haunches of a hare.

It found the pen, it was turning it over in its talons, thoughts were obviously moving around in its diseased brain, and then it fixed Alex with its bulging eyes and looked straight at him. Alex tried to tell himself that it couldn't see him, but it seemed to figure out where the pen had come from. It began to sniff tentatively in his direction. Alex began to hope for the policeman to start making a noise so that it would get them and not him and although he hated himself for the thought, he couldn't make it go away.

The creature's nose twitched like mad, it was trying to locate Alex by smell, still moving towards his position. Alex looked imploringly at Courtney with the policeman, but all he saw in their faces was resignation that he was lost. The thing's eyes had cleared, its pupils large, it could see again.

Alex could saw the drool on its lips as it prepared to leap forward, the talon-like hands reached out and it was airborne. It landed on Alex with the weight of the world, its breath hot and putrid; its drool touched his lips and tasted of blood. It sank its now long teeth into his arm and started to rip.

Alex was pinned down and terrified then suddenly covered in blood and bits of bone, half the creature's head was missing where the bullets had torn into its temple.

Chapter 2

Daniel Mason watched as the whaling ship gained on its prey, only a few more seconds and they would launch their deadly catapult into the flank of the fleeing whale. The bow of the Greenpeace ship, The Cafistan, crossed in front of the whaler causing it to veer to the side. Not as much as Daniel had hoped though, the ship struck the smaller vessel which a crack that felt like Daniel's own bones had broken. The Cafistan limped away, the damage to her side not as bad as it had sounded.

Daniel looked down from the whaler where he had been under cover for the last few weeks. In all that time they had managed to keep the whaler on the wrong track, always giving its position and a chance to move any whales from the area, until today.

The Humpbacks were only a hundred feet or so from the death ship and yet they had no desire to hurry away, they watched with interest at the crash of the two larger wooden whales.

Daniel considered his options. He would have to intercede for the whales or jump ship. Men on either side of him stood laughing and pointing down at the damaged Greenpeace ship as it limped away from him.

"Let us finish it," he heard in Russian. There were many Russians on board and yet he was not sure which nationality owned the ship. As a new member of the crew he had not been accepted enough for any information of interest. He had felt that they suspected him from the beginning but knew they would not have taken him along had this been true. it was just his natural paranoia kicking in, he had told himself.

The fact that he was an American and a vegan, the only one of either on board, had led to a certain amount of taunting from the older members of the crew. He had been tested and unwittingly been involved in a couple of fist fights that had left him with bruised ribs and swollen cheeks during his first few weeks with them. He had resisted using martial arts and taken the beating instead, though the second time he used just enough force to break the man's nose which made the others respect him.

The harpoon gun was aimed at the first Humpback as it breached the water.

"Let us take care of these pesky hippies while we can," it was a Russian voice again.

"Let us get on with the task in hand," Daniel spoke with authority in Russian, the Germans seem to understand also. They waved dismissive hands at the other ship and took their places for the slaughter to come.

Daniel made his way to the harpoon. The man aiming it was about a foot smaller though he was much thicker set. Daniel tapped him on the shoulder, then as he turned he punched him on the nose and pushed him away from the harpoon.

All the men seemed to be aware of him now, they started to bear down, Daniel pulled a gun from his back pocket and held it on them.

"No-one moves forward," he said again in Russian. He repeated it in German.

Two men were already moving towards him. He shot one in the leg and the other stopped.

"What are you doing?," the captain had appeared, he spoke in English with a clipped accent.

"I can hold you until the whales move on and my friends are further away," he fired another shot into the leg of someone moving towards him from the side.

"You mad man! You are insane, if you wait for the ship to go, how will you escape?"

"I'll be taking you into custody then." Daniel realized how stupid that sounded as he said it. These men weren't about to let him take them to any authorities, this was an illegal whaling boat with an international crew of cutthroats and thieves. As soon as they could overpower him, they would kill him. He glanced towards the ocean, it did not look too rough, but how far would he get?

The Greenpeace ship was not moving as fast as he wanted but the whales had gone away.

The two men whom he had shot in the legs still lay on the deck moaning about their wounds and calling to their shipmates for help. Daniel did not want to kill anyone, although he knew he would if he had to.

He glanced over the side again and realized he would rather take his chances in the cold rough water than stay here to be beaten and killed.

The captain saw his glance and laughed.

"So you think you are going to just swim away after this? Perhaps your little whale friends will carry you to safety. This is what you get from eating too many vegetables, my friend, a brain like a carrot."

Daniel wondered if he could get them all below deck and then lock them in, then he could signal to the Greenpeace ship, the Cafistan, to return and some of them could help him crew this ship back to the authorities. None of this had gone down like it was supposed to. He had been working undercover now for nearly six months, even Greenpeace didn't know that he was really FBI. His mission had been to track and identify the leaders of a smuggling ring that dealt with endangered species all over the world. As a vegan with a strong pro animal conviction he had been the perfect choice, or so they had thought. He had been under strict orders not to act until he had established who the ringleader was and where the finance came from. The lives of the whales before him would seem insignificant to many of his colleagues back in Boston but he couldn't stand by and watch them slaughtered. He had already ascertained that the captain of this ship was closely connected with the endangered species ring, though he had yet to discover the identity of the moneymen. His bosses were not going to be happy but it was too late now. His cover was blown, he watched the whales swim off into the distance and smiled. He had not yet reached his twenty third birthday and he suspected he never would.

"I hope you have something to smile about," the captain said, his eyes had a dark glaze around them. He was an older man, around fifty and there weren't too many of those around now. Whatever had killed people in the plague had seemed to target the over fifties. Some say there was something in the rain that had done it, no other explanation for a world-wide epidemic like it had been found.

"Killing a federal officer would mean the death sentence," Daniel said suddenly. Perhaps if they knew who he was they would not try to resist. On the other hand telling them was probably the biggest mistake he could have made. The moment the words left his mouth he regretted them. In trying to save his own life he now knew that he had sentenced the crew of the Cafistan to death. If they killed him, they would have to track it down and kill everyone on board just to make sure that there were no witnesses.

"I thought you were no ordinary veggie," the captain now regarded him with a hard glint in his eye. "Perhaps we can make a deal in the circumstances."

"I'm listening," Daniel desperately wanted to reload the gun.

"I don't think you want to kill us, you would prefer to take us in alive, plus there are twenty of us. You could not shoot us all."

"No," Daniel aimed the gun at the captain. "But you know I would take you out first and not with a bullet in the leg. I suggest that you move your men below deck, all of them."

Two men lunged forward slightly from the side, another from the middle, the captain had dropped and rolled out of the line of fire.

Daniel shot the first in the hip and the second in the leg, the third was almost on him and was killed at point blank range. It was not the first time Daniel had killed someone but it made his hand shake as it brought back the first time back to him, he pushed the memory away.

He looked for the captain but could not see him, the men were standing in front of him, shielding him. Loyalty or fear at what would happen to them if he was hurt, Daniel wondered.

Only one bullet remained in the gun, he knew it and they knew it. He wanted to make sure the captain got it, he had to be the target for that last bullet.

Someone moved suddenly on his left and for a moment he turned his full attention there as something hit him from above. A searing pain shot down his back as he went down on the deck, a sand bag landed next to him. He tried to get up but they were on him already, he felt a couple of kicks to his stomach and then it went dark.

As he drifted he thought back to his first undercover assignment, the one where he had been forced to kill. His mind floated above the action as he relived the minutes over and over in his sleep. For all he knew this was the end for him, they might not intend for him to wake up and he would be forever caught in the hell of his subconscious.

Her name had been Dallentry, Victoria Dallentry. Her family were wealthy and heavily involved in illegal arms sale to Middle Eastern countries. As part of his mission, he had befriended her at a Beverley Hills tennis club. A thin plain girl with a gawky smile, barely eighteen. Her parents had already spent large amounts of money trying to get her face changed so that it fit in with their beautiful people lifestyle. She was practically an outcast in the family and a perfect target for the FBI. Daniel had shown considerable interest in her, though never crossing the line. It had taken him some time to gain her trust but in doing so, he also found her to be a charming and clever girl. He liked the way her mind worked and was determined to make sure that she did not get hurt by his investigation into her father. She wanted to spend more and more time with him and had finally invited him to their fortified mansion for dinner. He came across as a clean cut American, the same age as her, too young to be a threat. He appeared to be a good student, was intelligent and had a certain charm about his looks. Unfortunately this last quality sparked an immediate distrust in Victoria's father, Belos, who could not believe that anyone could be interested in Victoria for herself.

Aros and Carn, Victoria's brothers, were present for dinner but her mother was absent. Victoria was sad by this as it was her beautiful mother that she had really wanted Daniel to meet. A special liver dish was offered for first course along with stilted conversation and an uneasy atmosphere which Daniel's attempts at levity failed to change. The main course was a beautiful roast beef which hardly anyone touched and a whiskey cream cheesecake for dessert.

After dinner Belos asked to see Daniel in his study which was large and sparsely furnished plus curiously devoid of books. Daniel sat down as requested in a large winged chair in the middle of the room while Belos circled around him. A cross examination had been expected but if Daniel could just get through it, he would be able to complete his mission that night and find the proof required.

"Daniel, you are something of an enigma to me," Belos said in his strange whiney voice. He had a constant cough and an unpleasant face.

"I'm just a friend of your daughter sir," Daniel replied respectfully. "I have the greatest regard for Victoria as a friend. I can assure you that my intentions are honourable," the last word almost caught in his throat and doom hovered in the air around him.

"I know who you say you are," Belos continued "but I also know who you really are, an undercover cop, sent here to connect me to various ....activities. You are so young too. These days they will train anyone who makes it through school. Was your father a policeman?"

Daniel's blood ran cold, he went to stand up from the chair and found that the two brothers were now holding him there.

"Look I don't know where your information comes from but..."

"I know you aren't wearing a wire and anyway all radio frequencies are blocked in this house. I know you have no back up and that your mission was to gain access to the house. Many other things I know also."

"How do you know them?" Daniel asked. He was unarmed and unsupported.

"I have someone in the bureau that lets me know these things. Unfortunately for both of us, my contacts know as well and are most displeased that this has happened. It has been decided that the weakness in my family must be eradicated before it brings further disgrace." The door opened and Victoria walked in, she moved in front of Daniel and he could see her face change from fear to horror as she began to comprehend what was about to happen to him.

"Father, why are you doing this?" Her voice was small and shy. She walked towards him but he moved away.

18

"He is a spy my dear. Not interested in you, just what you can do for him."

"A spy, a spy for who? Why would anyone want to spy on me?"

"Dense as well as ugly," her father said, she recoiled. Daniel wanted to jump up, to defend her, to tell them all to stop picking on her, but he did not move.

"I'm not either. Mother would never allow you to call me those things."

"Ah yes," Belos moved to Daniel who struggled suddenly to no avail. "Your mother is the price I had to pay for your refusal to obey me. Your mother, who was taken from me this morning. They came and killed her as a warning. Then they made us serve her liver as an appetizer. If we don't make things right, they will kill us all. But I intend to give you a choice too." Belos opened the desk drawer and took out a long knife, practically a sword. Ornate with blue stones in the handle and a gold line running along the blade.

"Take this Victoria and become our avenger. Plunge the blade into this man's heart that has deprived us of your mother and brought the wrath of my partners upon us."

He offered out the knife but Victoria backed away, her brothers watched with growing unease and for a second their concentration was only on her, Aros started to be sick, they hadn't known about the liver.

Daniel flipped his feet up and grabbed Aros by the neck flicking him into Carn. As they went down he grabbed the gun from Aros and rolled away from them. Belos reached into the desk again so Daniel shot him in the knee. He turned and fired leg shots into the other two brothers. They all seemed incapacitated but other guards were at the door. He picked up the phone and dialled for back up, they were in a van a couple of blocks away and would be there in under three minutes, Belos contact had not known everything.

Daniel made sure that there were no weapons around, he felt sick himself but he cast his thoughts away from it. He wanted to comfort Victoria, his heart was overwhelmed with pity as she stood, her face blank and white, her lip trembling, the knife hanging from her hand.

She looked from her father to her brothers and back. All at once she screamed and swung the knife out at her father catching him across the throat. She screamed for her mother and slashed him again.

Daniel found himself screaming at her to stop, he raised his gun and warned her. She turned towards him seeming to fly, her face contorted with grief and madness. He shot her in the leg but she felt no pain, and was on him. She thrust the knife deep into his shoulder. He pushed her back but she took the knife with her and was on him again but not before he had shot her in the heart at point blank range. Then he screamed.

Daniel awoke in the hold, from his usual nightmare to a new kind, he could still hear screaming, high pitched, shrill as if people were being torn apart above him on deck. Before he had a chance to wonder what he was doing in the hold, he heard the footsteps dragging themselves towards him.

Chapter 3

Alex woke up with his head and shoulder bandaged. The room was small, with paint such a bright blue, that for a moment he thought he had died and was floating above the clouds. His eyes hurt from the glare. A uniformed guard was sitting against the far wall. He had noticed the awakening and immediately jumped up to fetch the others. Alex tried to move and was suddenly aware that his arms and legs were clamped to the bed. Over on his left near the window, a shotgun was fixed to the wall, the notice above it said "Emergency use."

Alex was still staring at the gun when three men dressed in white walked in. They stood around the bed gaping at him as though he was the last thing they expected to see in the bed.

"Could you loosen these bonds doctor?" Alex said, surprisingly coherently since his tongue appeared to belong in someone else's mouth.

"How do you feel?" The tallest man was speaking, he had a long beard which Alex was sure would get in the way of administering medicine; he was most un-doctor like.

"I feel okay" Alex didn't sound it; his voice was weak and cracked. "You are doctors aren't you?

The tall man moved a little closer, though he glanced towards the shotgun before he did so. Alex began to find the whole thing a little amusing, not only had he had an adventure in the Twilight Zone, he was now living in it.

"My Name is Seth Richards, I am a professor of archaeology from America. These are doctors, Wilson and Kerrigan." The doctor that spoke had obvious authority about him. He was younger than the others but clearly in charge.

Alex looked from one to the other, "Are any of you medical doctors?" Seth Richards did not look like a doctor, he was only a few years older than Alex and there was a hardness around his eyes, a glacial quality that made him look intimidating.

"Do you feel sick?" Asked Richards.

"Do I feel… just what is going on here? Where am I?" Alex was feeling better and the more he talked the more his tongue felt like his own.

"Mr Cartier, we need to be perfectly candid with you. We believe that you have been infected with a virus, a virus that will eventually kill you. It is our job to study you and if possible to use the information you can relay to us to help stop this happening to other people. We don't have time to play games, the virus you have works in five stages. You are presently in the second stage where we may talk to you. If you will tell us everything about how you are feeling you will greatly help our research"

Alex was looking around the room as he listened to the doctor. A new sensation had begun to fill his body and his mind. Self-preservation. The need to be free was becoming suddenly important to him. His lack of attention was noted by the surrounding doctors.

"Did you hear what I said to you?"

"Of course," Alex returned his attention back to the scientist "I'm not deaf." He shifted in the bed suddenly feeling uncomfortable. "I am dying with some strange disease and you want to study me. Why are you are in here if this thing is so catching?"

Dr Wilson, a short man with bright ginger hair glanced up at the ceiling. "It can only be passed through saliva or blood exchange. However, we do have a force field in place," he shuffled his feet, "latest thing" he added.

Alex looked up at the ceiling and saw a line of small light bulbs encompassing his bed. Directly overhead, almost camouflaged, was a square machine. Now that he focussed on it, Alex could hear it making a faint whirring sound.

Dr Wilson followed his gaze "You see that machine provides your oxygen, the surrounding emitters keep your oxygen from mixing with ours, just in case. Very high tech," the man forced a smile again as if he thought this would put Alex at ease.

"Very Star Trek," Alex said dryly. "I don't see how that stops you from getting infected though."

"You can't infect us unless your blood or spit mix with ours, this prevents that, prevents you from attacking us," Wilson said in his upbeat way.

Alex sighed. "You said I was in stage two, how long does that last?" Alex shifted around on the bed; it made the doctors uncomfortable they all glanced at the gun.

Alex laughed, "Look, I'm not dangerous, I don't know what's going on but I think you've made a mistake. I'm a banker I work at …." Alex had forgotten where he worked. A searing pain exploded in his head and without thinking he put his hand up to it. The restraint snapped. The doctors flew out of the room as did the armed guard. An alarm started to sound then the wall in front of the bed slid away to reveal a glass panel. The doctors were soon on the other side of it.

Wilson spoke into a microphone, his voice filled Alex's room.

"Sorry Alex, Phase three has come into effect before schedule. We can do nothing but observe."

The pain had gone from Alex's head, he looked at the broken bond on his wrist and pulled at the other one, it snapped very easily. Next he undid his ankles, he was aware of the force field still surrounding the bed.

"You don't intend to keep me on this bed the whole time do you? I'm hungry anyway. I also have a lot of influential friends who won't be too happy at this treatment of me."

Wilson looked very agitated at this statement. Richards took over the microphone. "What would you like to eat?" it sounded like a test question.

"Breakfast would be nice. Cereal, milk, some toast?" He kicked at the covers, "gin and tonic," he said under his breath.

He felt surprisingly in good spirits. Instead of feeling angry, scared, confused, he felt the best he ever had. "Any chance of a mirror? I'd like to shave."

"Can't give you any weapons, sorry." As an afterthought, "perhaps we could get you a mirror."

"Thanks." Alex had the impulse to feel his face, to make sure it hadn't changed; he remembered the thing from the previous night and had no wish to look like it. Although he now remembered the events that had led him here, he had no feelings about them. He no longer felt fear when he thought of that horrible creature and the fact that it had somehow infected him with a virus, probably when it drooled on him or ripped his arm almost off. Though his arm seemed okay, as if it were completely undamaged.

Life was starting to look different, his attitudes were changing. His mind was changing. Phase four, he wondered.

"Has a real doctor seen me?" He was talking to Wilson through the glass. For some reason he liked Wilson, the other two he did not. "Don't you think that if I have a virus someone should be doing something to get it out of me?"

"What do you want to eat?" Richards asked his eyes intent, his expression expectant.

Alex kicked at the bedclothes, "I thought we established this already. Is there a problem with the cereal? You tell me what's on the menu and I'll choose something else."

The wall went back into place and he suddenly felt alone. He reached for the bedclothes and nearly slid off the bed, he waved his hand without thinking outside the perimeter force field and immediately wished he had not. A bright pain seared through his hand as it recoiled involuntarily back to his side. The pain was so intense that his eyes filled with water and a spasm hit his whole body. He examined his hand to find his fingers all singed and a hole straight through the middle of it. He screamed out some expletive and waited for the wall to disappear again. His captors, however, remained shy or perhaps they had some other surprise to cook up for him he thought.

He lay on the bed for some time just thinking, he wasn't sure how long, it was almost like a trance where time meant nothing. He came back to his senses as the door opened and someone entered wearing a yellow space suit.

"Don't be alarmed." The voice was female.

"Why should I be?" Alex waved his damaged hand at her. "I have a hole in my—" He broke off. His hand had almost completely healed. The hole was gone and just a few abrasions remained. Even those seemed to be disintegrating before his eyes.

"I hurt my hand," he waved it at her again, it was impossible to see her face under that visor. "I'm not dangerous. Are you a doctor?" Alex continued

"No, Mr Cartier, I am with British Intelligence."

"Really? Well that's good, I'm sure the others don't have any. I was with British Intelligence till a couple of years ago, you know. Don't you have a record of me?"

"Yes, I've seen your file. Just the one mission wasn't it?" Her voice was sweet, even under the mask. "You were recruited at school. Very young"

Alex went silent, she did know about him, she had already weighed him up and decided that he had never taken the service seriously.

"My name is Samantha Wells. You can call me Sam if you like." She moved nearer to him but did not glance up at the laser projectors.

"Don't come too close. You could get a nasty scratch," he almost stretched his hand out without thinking but quickly withdrew it.

"This should have all been explained to you Alex. This bed is surrounded by a laser power force field. You must not cross its border or it will kill you."

Alex looked at the video camera in the corner; they hadn't seen him burn himself. They had been doing something else after all. Wouldn't they get a surprise when they watched the tapes?

"I'm a quick healer." He could almost make her face out now through the face plate, blue eyes, pretty mouth. "I feel perfectly okay, I'm sure that this is all unnecessary, perhaps I'm immune to it."

"It?" She had edged nearer.

"The virus or whatever." Anyway, I still need to eat and possibly use the bathroom at some point. A clock would be good to. I've no idea how long I've been here. Could be days"

"You've only been awake for a little over an hour."

"How long has it been since they offered me breakfast?" Alex rubbed his hand, how quickly had it healed.

"About ten minutes. I'm sorry you were left alone for that time. I want to assure you that we appreciate your help in dealing with this thing."

Alex was silent for a moment. His hand was as good as new. A virus with healing properties, no wonder British Intelligence was interested. "Any sign of the food," he said lightly "I can't tell you when I've felt so hungry."

"Your food is coming. You still want , cereal and toast?"

"I don't care anymore." He slumped back in the bed. He no longer felt hungry, just angry that they wouldn't feed him. After all he was their guinea pig. "What happened to the girl I was with, Cassandra? Does she know I'm here?"

"All the people that were at the party last night have been contacted and have been tested for any creature contact. We believe that you were the only one infected, the only one that survived anyway."

Alex snorted. "So Cassandra is okay? I really don't think that I've been infected by that thing. I feel great."

A ceiling panel opened abruptly over his head and a tray started to descend towards him. He could see through the panel an armed guard pointing a weapon at him yet he still felt calm and in good spirits and that in itself sent a shiver down his spine.

The tray had reached a good height for him to eat off. He lifted the silver lid to find frosted cereal, toast, and, on a side plate, a raw steak. He glanced over to the girl. She was already by the door ready to leave. The panel in the wall opened up and the scientists practically pushed their noses against the glass. Something was expected of him.

"Thanks," he said and started to eat the cereal. "Very nice."

Having a bloody raw piece of meat on the tray had no effect on his appetite.

He finished the cereal and looked up to the armed guard.

"Okay take her away." The tray began to ascend until it was gone and the panel closed behind it.

"Perhaps if you tell me what's going on, I might be able to help you," his hand waved out and the fingers caught the edge of the laser. Alex pulled his hand back straight away but although he had seen the laser hit the fingers, he had not felt it.

"Let me see your hand," the girl was distressed, " I'll call in a medical team. You need to have your arms by your side so that accidents like that don't happen. The restraints would have stopped this."

"I'm fine. Really."

"But your fingers, the beam would have taken them off…." She could see they were intact as he waved them at her. "I don't understand."

Alex had an impulse and thrust his hand into the laser. The laser penetrated his hand without damage. His limb was healing itself quicker than it was being damaged. His body had learnt how to deal with the laser.

He decided to take this opportunity to show he meant no harm and swung his legs over the side of the bed. Standing up was easier than he had thought, he moved towards the girl with his hands held out in what he hoped was a friendly action. She bolted for the door but he was there before her in the wisp of a second. He pulled her mask off and stared down into her bright frightened eyes. The panel opened in the ceiling and a gun was aimed at him.

"Hey just calm down" he shouted towards the soldier looking through the hatch. More armed men had appeared through the window. Clearly no one knew what to do. Odd that he could now hear them through the toughened glass.

"How are we going to hold him" he could hear Richards whisper. "Tell them to take a shot."

"What about Samantha?" The voice belonged to Wilkins.

"They won't hit her, he may have compromised her anyway.
"

Alex pushed Sam away from him. "Look she's okay, I haven't drooled on her or anything, I just want to speak to someone in charge."

"Take him!" He heard the cry as the soldier opened fire from the ceiling. Quickly he threw himself under the bed. As he had thought, the bed was made of some sort of heavy metal, the bullets weren't penetrating it. He looked across to Samantha, she had thrown herself on the floor but the bullets were flying everywhere, eventually she would be hit. So much for take a shot. He couldn't just pull her under the bed, she would be killed by the lasers. He rolled out, caught three bullets in his shoulder, and covered her with his body then used his own flesh as a shield against the lasers to get her under the bed. He hardly felt the lasers ripping into his back but he did feel extreme pain as the bullets entered his body. His shoulder looked almost ripped off. The men had stopped firing, Sam was lying quietly underneath him, she did not appear to be wounded just scared to death.

A minute or so went by and his shoulder no longer hurt, the flesh had already knitted together and popped the bullets out as it did so. He wondered what could be taking them so long to decide what to do? A minute is a long time when you are trapped under a reinforced steel bed with people trying to kill you on all sides. At least the bullets couldn't penetrate the laser border around the bed, they were destroyed as they went through it. Then he realized, they were waiting for the laser to be turned off, his only chance was to communicate with them

"Richards!" No he didn't like Richards. "Wilson! I was just trying to show that I meant no harm."

"Why have you got the girl?" Richards had answered.

"To stop your men from killing her, you bast***." He regretted using a swear word, it probably would not endear himself to them and Richards did unfortunately appear to be in control.

"We don't want to kill anyone," it was Wilson. "We want to help you."

The force field dropped. Guns were reloading.

"I don't have any animosity towards you people. Let me at least send out the girl"

"Why? Because you have contaminated her?"

"No, because she is one of yours."

He could hear whispering, Richards was getting men ready to storm the door, Wilson was arguing. He really liked Wilson.

"We could kill him and just wound her, she should be okay." Richards was saying.

"You're forgetting who she is," Wilson responded.

"It might be best to kill him and see what we can find out through autopsy." Richards continued. "And I could never forget who she is."

"Who the hell are you people? Don't you understand that we're all right, we're not infected? Give me a break."

"He can hear what we're saying," it was Wilson "Take him out now while we still can."

"Wilson! Come on I could be your only hope to beat this." Alex watched the door expecting men to fly through it at any second. His best bet was through the glass, but he couldn't take the girl that way and for some reason he wanted to take her. She was unconscious and there was some blood on her head. Perhaps she had been shot before he got her under the bed. She moved her arm and mumbled something.

The door burst open and a man with a rocket launcher stood there but before he could fire, Alex was across the room and knocked him to the ground.

"I just want to talk!" he called out. "Don't make me really hurt someone."

A hail of machine gun fire hit him in the back but his body had already dealt with this before and healed on impact. The healing was so fast that it looked as if the bullets were bouncing off. He dashed back to collect the girl and then leapt with her through the open hatch into the ceiling knocking the men with guns from the area. He couldn't tell how hard he was knocking them; he just hoped that they weren't being killed.

"I don't want to do this," he kept shouting.

Inside the hatch room he closed the trap door and lay the girl on the floor, she was becoming conscious again.

"What's happening?"

He looked at her blankly. "How the hell should I know? Do you know a way out of here?"

"You mustn't get out of here," she said and reached into her pocket and produced a grenade. She pulled the pin and dropped it to the floor.

"What the…" Alex knocked her away as softly as he could; gaging his new strength was difficult. He threw himself onto the grenade, he didn't know why, he just had to, for her.

As it went off he was flung over to the far wall, hit it with a thud and slid down to the floor. His insides were hanging out from his body. Why had he thought he could sustain that sort of injury? It hurt like mad, the room was dimming around him as he held his stomach in he could feel a piece of the grenade inside.

"I don't understand" he said as more soldiers burst through the door their weapons opened fire and riddled his chest. The girl screamed.

Chapter 4

Daniel found himself tied and gagged, leant against the store room wall. The door was closed and he supposed, locked.

He was surprised to have woken up at all and he wondered how the Greenpeace ship had faired. Perhaps it had escaped and they couldn't risk killing him immediately.

His head and mouth hurt, plus it felt as though his ankle may be broken. He winced as he tried to move it but continued to struggle with the rope on his wrists.

The screaming continued above and the footsteps had reached the door. It swung open and the captain stood in front of him leaning a little to the side. His eyes were bright and darted around the room alighting on his face occasionally as if he couldn't control his gaze. He lurched forward and sat down abruptly on the floor opposite Daniel.

"Do you know what has happened?" He asked his tongue darting in and out like a large lizard in search of water.

"No but I have a feeling you are going to tell me." Daniel pushed himself away.

"Yes, I could tell you. After all, you may be my only hope of survival," He produced a large knife from out of his belt and pointed it towards Daniel.

"Your ankle is broken." He sniffed and waved the knife around. "I did it myself just a few minutes ago. You didn't even wake up so there was little joy in it for me."

"Oh I'm so sorry, no doubt you can make up for it now." Daniel watched the knife which the captain was aimlessly waving around.

"You're American aren't you? Your accent is showing."

"I see no further reason to hide it," Daniel said as he felt his bonds loosen a little. "You don't look so good."

"Don't I?" The captain slashed out with his knife and caught Daniel on his calf. "You don't look so good either," the captain chuckled. " Let me tell you what I intend to do with you. I am going to drink your blood. I don't want to, please don't think that I am some kind of vampire. I have to drink it to survive," he licked some of the blood from the knife, Daniel recoiled, he put his hand down to his leg and felt the warm blood pumping over it.

Daniel felt his hands loosen a bit more. His leg hurt now as much as his mouth but the blood flow was already stopping and the pain had been fleeting, there was no dull after ache.

"Your friends are not far from us, we will have caught up with them within an hour or two and when that happens, they will be slaughtered as my crew have been."

"Your crew?" Daniel watched as the captain pushed a large barrel across the doorway.

"You must know!" He was shouting, clasping the knife in his hand so hard that blood gushed through his fingers. Then Daniel realized that this man's behaviour was that of a cornered animal, terrified, aggressive and highly dangerous. Like a wolf with its paw already caught in the trap, he had accepted his fate and yet would fight it till the last breath left his body to be free.

"Your blood could be my salvation," his eyes were wild, he ran a hand through his hair and left large streaks of blood on his cheek.

"You've been drinking the seawater have you?" Daniel said. "Why didn't you kill me before?"

Suddenly their attention was taken by someone else outside the door, pushing it, testing the barrier. His hands were nearly free, if he could just buy a few more moments with some banal chatter he knew he could take the wild man in front of him despite his wounds and broken ankle.

The captain suddenly became calm, he seemed unaware of the door swaying to and fro behind him.

"Let me tell you what happened," the captain said through a cracked voice.

"I was about to put a bullet in your brain and toss you over the side, then catch up to your friends and dispose of each one of them but a wailing sound stopped me. It was so piercing that it actually made my head ache. We all turned to see where it was coming from and it turned out to be one of my own men. His body was changing before our eyes. His hair was falling from his head in great bloody clumps, his arms grew long and seemed to weigh much more than he was used to. To compensate, his backbone must have doubled in width to accommodate his new bulk."

Daniel wondered where this story was going but as his hands were now free, he was glad that he didn't have to find out. He lunged forward and wrenched the knife from the captain's hand, it was almost too easy. They stood up together until Daniel hit the wild man with a hook straight to the jaw, he heard it crack. The man went down and lay there wheezing and chuckling.

"There's no safety for you out there," the captain said through cracked teeth. "I am your only hope to get off this ship and you are mine but I'll only help you if you smear some of your blood on me and let me drink it."

"Oh I don't think that that is going to happen." Daniel wondered why the captain would continue with his bizarre story, unless he believed it to be true.

"My shipmate continued to change, it was so frightening and he looked in pain," the captain shrugged. "I had to shoot him. Despite that he started to grab at men, snapping their necks and throwing them around. I turned and made my way down below."

"You hid," Daniel said with some contempt still unsure as to the point of this fable.

"Yes, I'm no coward though, if that is what you are thinking. You didn't see these things."

"There were more than one?"

"Yes, there were many of them, at least four. I watched one of them carry you down here and leave you in this room, tied as you were. I came here and smashed your ankle with a piece of whaling equipment." The man broke off to chortle as if he had just told the best joke.

"You didn't even wake up and I wanted you to be awake when I killed you. Then I realized that there was something special to them about you. Here they were killing my men on deck, ripping their heads open and yet they left you in here, safe away from the carnage. I thought perhaps.."

"Perhaps if you drank my blood? Give me a break, oh I forgot you already did, for no apparent reason."

"I didn't want you to slip away amidst the chaos."

Daniel felt a nagging itch in his ankle and could not stop himself from reaching down and feeling the dislodged piece of bone. As he touched it, the boned seemed to recoil and jumped back into place, one jolt of pain and it was good as new.

He heard the sharp cry from the captain as what he had witnessed but he was too consumed with his own bewilderment. He looked at the wound inflicted on the shin that had already closed.

"What are you? I broke your ankle twice and each time it healed." The captain asked in a fearful voice, his eyes darting towards the door as if he would rather take his chances with the monsters outside than with Daniel.

"I was just an ordinary guy this morning, I don't know what's going on." A thought came over Daniel, he jammed the knife against the captain's rib cage.

"Did you drug me? Is this all a hallucination?"

The captain snorted, "If it was, would I be part of it. Moron."

Daniel felt very keen on killing him at that moment but he resisted the urge and backed off. The door had started to move again with more force than last time.

"Why didn't they kill you?" He flung at the captain, determined to find some rationality. His wounds were now completely healed.

"I don't know, they knew I was still around but they didn't see me sneak in here. I guess they kept me for the same reason they are pursuing your friends on the Cafistan. They eat brains, but judging what I saw. They like fresh ones."

"Okay, I don't need to meet them," Daniel stood back with his back to the wall facing the door. There was no doubt now that something had decided it was coming through and all he had was this knife.

He saw a sudden movement from the side as the captain launched himself but Daniel knocked him back effortlessly with the back of his hand. A scaly hand of fear had grabbed at his heart and was squeezing it in, making it pump much faster.

The door flew open and a bug eyed monster stood before him. The arms brushed along the floor, there was blood around the mouth and chin, the teeth jagged, the eyes pitted and black, it looked blind.

"It can't see us." The captain said from the floor where he had pushed himself behind a box as the creature broke the door down. The thing immediately swung its head towards the captain's position but remained motionless.

That was an intelligent move, Daniel thought, give it your position.

They stood sometime like that, the creature blocking the doorway, the men too afraid to move. Daniel could see others behind the first, their eyes also dark and unseeing. They just appeared to be waiting.

A few moments went by, Daniel was just wondering about hacking at the wooden wall with his knife when the dark eyes suddenly cleared and the creatures could see. The one at the front fixed Daniel with its new gaze and seemed to nod then it sought out the captain and pulled him to his feet. All the time he was screaming and cursing as the monster tossed him almost over his shoulder, like a rag doll he was passed to the creatures waiting behind who took him out of hearing range.

Daniel prepared the knife for battle and himself for death, the creature was coming for him now.

It stopped just in front of him and the others made a path for him, it appeared that they wanted him to walk through them but they were not forcing him. He gathered his courage, which had scattered completely and moved forward, the knife held firmly in his hand. He made his way up on deck as they seemed to want. He was horrified to see the Greenpeace ship only a hundred feet from his own. It was not moving and people were on deck, probably watching in horror through binoculars, unable to believe what they were seeing. He wondered why they weren't moving, perhaps they realized they could not outrun it.

Over on the other side of the deck he saw the captain. He was on his knees with two other people from his crew. They were surrounded by six or seven creatures, another four were behind Daniel. The rest of the crew were gone, all that remained of them were bloody stains on the darkened deck.

He assumed that they wanted him to join the other prisoners but as he moved towards them, the monsters became agitated so he stopped.

"My name is special agent Daniel Mason, FBI." It's all right now because I'm the guy form the FBI. A song which he had made up while on training with his buddies kept running through his mind.

Just keep calm, you are safe now.

The men in black will take a bow

Don't fear the bullet or the knife,

We'll protect your children and your wife,

Never fear I'm the guy from the FBI.

He felt sick in his stomach, all attention was now on him, the captain had a faint smile on his lips.

"I want these people released and put into that boat over there," He indicated a small rowboat which could be lowered into the water. He intended to join it and get the hell out of dodge.

"Release them immediately," he waved his knife in the general direction of the prisoners.

"Put him in the boat. You're all under arrest." He wasn't sure why he continued speaking but he saw no other option.

Where he had indicated the boat, one of the creatures had gone over to it and was sniffing around it in great breaths.

Daniel indicated the captain, "Put him in the boat with the others."

They seemed to understand and harshly lifted the captain up tossing him from one to the other, like a bag of flour, until he landed firmly in the boat with a thwack. Daniel moved to the boat, it looked as though it would not be too difficult to lower it into the water.

Nobody leaves this ship, you all stay here." Daniel was feeling weak, his strength ebbed for a moment and he thought he might collapse, then he felt stronger than ever.

The creatures picked up another of the men and tossed him along the line throwing him into the boat like they were a sack of rations.

"Okay good. Now just one more." Daniel indicated the last man but to no avail. There seemed to be some sort of silent conversation going on between the creatures. They were not happy at parting with their last trophy.

Daniel raised his voice, "Get him in the boat!"

The creatures moved themselves into a huddle as if they were in a boardroom discussing something. One of them came out from the middle and bowed to Daniel. Yes there was no mistake this time, it had bowed to him. It was looking deep into his eyes and he could understand its human like voice echoing in his mind.

"We can't give you all the food. There will be more for you on the other ship. We smell them from here, maybe ten or fifteen people. Take these and leave us if you must, we will meet again."

Daniel was filled by horror, could it understand his thoughts? From the vacant expression on its face, he assumed not.

"Go to them and seek out those that are like you" the voice was in his brain again.

"I demand that you release that man over there and consider yourselves all under arrest."

"Forget it Clarice and get in the damn boat," the captain's voice was harsh behind him. Two of the creatures had moved to the boat and were ready with their long arms to hoist it over the side and lower it with the ropes.

Daniel looked at the remaining prisoner. He was bleeding on the forehead. His hands were tied behind him and his jaw looked broken. Daniel looked at his face. It was the harpoon operator, Mollen. Daniel's thoughts reflected back to how he had considered Mollen less than a human, how he had heard about Mollen killing a man in a bar just for getting his drink before him. Mollen looked at him with beseeching eyes. He mouthed the words "help me."

Mollen was not worth making a stand for, Daniel knew that, but he was caught by his honour despite his loathing for the man, he could not just walk away and leave him to be butchered.

"He goes with us," Daniel tried to sound as confident as possible. The creatures moved around uneasily. Something was happening to them again, their arms were losing some of their length, hair was growing on their slimy overgrown heads which appeared to be shrinking. They started to have a vague humanoid look about them.

"Let's go," hissed the captain.

The creature in front of him glanced at one of the guards of the remaining prisoner, it nodded and ripped his head off. The body slumped to the ground, the head was given to one of the others and taken below.

"Do you still want it?" The voice in his brain was asking. The voice was wary now though, almost as if it sensed that they had made a mistake with him.

Daniel said nothing, he backed up to the boat and got in. For a moment he thought that the creatures would kill them all but they started to lower the boat into the water and soon they rowed in silence to towards the Cafistan.

Daniel wondered where the whaling ship would go now, whether it would return to dock or travel the seas looking for unsuspecting travellers to prey on.

The captain and the other man were rowing as fast as they could. Neither of them looked very good, their colour was pallid, their lips white. Daniel recalled what he had been told about the first one, that it had been one of the men and then suddenly turned. He looked at the remnants of clothing hanging from the grotesquely shaped creatures and realized that these monsters had once been the crew that he had known. They had somehow changed into beast-like creatures, were still changing. He glanced at the two men rowing again and wondered how long it would be before they changed or perhaps like him, they were immune.

When they reached the Greenpeace boat Daniel called for his case to brought to the boat and lowered down. He didn't want anyone coming in contact with the men in the boat.

His case was duly lowered down and he extracted two pairs of handcuffs from the false bottom. He was aware that the people above were watching, people who he had deceived for some time. They had thought he was there for his love of animals not for the government.

After the two men were secure Daniel climbed up onto the deck. Ten worried faces looked at him with hurt expressions, they glanced nervously from one to another. No doubt his cover was blown.

"I am with the FBI," he said as calmly as possible. The captain was shouting from the boat below. Daniel moved everyone below deck.

Once in the main cabin he continued. "I haven't betrayed any of you, I'm not here for any of you." He knew there were pot smokers on board and people with mysterious pasts and wanted to put their minds at rest.

"I was working undercover to stop the illegal slaughter of whales and to investigate the murder of two agents that disappeared last year. While on the other boat, something terrible and strange has happened. The men with me may be contagious with some sort of disease. They are not to be brought on board or to have any contact with anyone here. I will tend to them myself."

"You can't drag them along in that boat, it won't keep up," Jamie piped up. He had been a friend of Daniel while they were on the Greenpeace ship. Jamie had helped him get aboard the whaling vessel.

"I might bring them on board later," Daniel replied. "But no-one can be around if I do."

"They need medical attention don't they," Katrina asked. A Spanish girl with long dark hair and bright green eyes. Daniel had felt sure that she had been attracted to him before, he had almost fallen under her influence but his ethics had kept him clear. Now she looked at him as if he was a foreigner whom she was having trouble understanding.

These people meant well but they weren't terribly fond of the authorities, especially the FBI who had interfered with them on occasion. To actually have been used in some sting operation must have been very difficult for them to forgive.

44

"I don't think that medicine will help," Daniel said as gently as he could.

"What have you done Daniel?" The elder man, Larry Roman was looking deeply concerned.

"What have I done?" Daniel took a good look at the faces that surrounded him. They were frightened and their eyes darted to his hand every now and then. He looked down and saw that he still held the knife, held it so tightly that his knuckles were white. His own blood had stained it red where he had been wounded.

"Oh, it's my blood," he indicated his leg, there was no wound on his leg.

"Let me take the knife," Larry moved forward and held out his hand.

"Fine, I don't need it." Daniel still had his bag in the other hand and buried in the bottom was a nice gun.

Larry took the knife and everyone seemed to relax. Katrina went over to him and laid her palm on his cheek. She did still like him he thought.

"Okay, let's get those men up and see what we can do for them," Larry had taken control.

"No!" Daniel pushed forward. "They are dangerous, they have to stay where they are. I should have left them behind or killed them." He hadn't meant to say the last part out loud but everyone heard it.

"I think you need to rest," Larry continued. "Katrina take him to my cabin."

"No!" Daniel pushed Katrina away with more force than he meant to and she slipped on the floor. He moved forward to help her up but was grabbed by the men behind. He started to struggle but they had him down on the floor and a weakness had come over him again, four of them sat on him, keeping him still while they injected him with something.

"Oh no, don't put me to sleep. I'll wake up and you'll all be dead, I'll be surrounded by monsters, you'll turn into monsters!"

"Ssh, you will be okay," it was Katrina by his ear, then he was asleep.

He slumped on the ground and was carried to the cabin.

While he slept the captain and the other man were brought on board and taken to the infirmary. They were still handcuffed to the beds, Larry wasn't going to take any chances with them. Especially since he recognized the captain as a man of extreme corruption who he knew to be as much a monster as Daniel thought he could be.

"Come on don't leave me in the same room with Teloni, he's not well!" The captain had become aware that his shipmate was beginning to look far worse than on the boat.

"Someone will be outside the door," Larry said and left.

The captain lay there for a while watching with small frightened eyes for any change in Teloni. It was less than an hour later when he noticed that the fingernails had grown, more than that, he could actually see them growing.

Chapter 5

And death shall come, but not for you my son, for you are unique and must remain here always.

Alex opened his eyes and focussed slowly on the room about him. Grey unpainted walls, no windows and a heavy iron door greeted his lingering gaze. His head pounded to the beat of some nineties rock song and his limbs ached in unison. He had no memory. His name, life and the events of the last few days had been wiped away which left him feeling vulnerable and afraid. He pushed the covers back and swung himself up from the bed. His legs reacted immediately, the ache leaving them, his arms felt strength returning to them and his brain kicked into life. A hundred thousand visions flooded back to him in one tidal wave of emotion, which knocked him to the floor. He remembered everything now. He also remembered that he should be dead.

As the visions in his mind receded he found himself at the iron door. There was no handle on his side; it looked like it probably had a special locking mechanism activated from outside the grey room. He looked around for a video camera but could not see one, nor did the wall look as if it might glide away and reveal a flock of scientists ready to begin their examination.

He looked for any sign of wounds on his body and found none. There were no surgery marks where his intestine would have been pushed back in and his shoulder showed no signs of scarring where it had been lacerated to the bone.

He thought of the girl, Samantha, had she survived was she in the next room or cold in her grave?

A rumbling sound on the door caught his attention as the door opened outward, a man he recognized entered. It was Courtney, the man from the hotel that had almost saved his life.

"Alex, it's good to see you awake and moving around. We were quite fearful for your life. I know I owe you an explanation but you have to understand first that you are an exception to a new rule. We are at a loss as to why you are not affected in the same way as others but it is now clear to us that you are not."

"What the hell are you talking about?" Alex moved towards Courtney but saw no fear in the old man's eyes. "What others?"

"Sit down Alex. I will tell you what has happened in the last six months since you have been here."

"Six months!" Every fibre of his body stood on end and cried out at once.

"Yes, we have kept you sedated for much of the time. It was not until today that you were allowed to wake up," Courtney looked away as he said allowed and Alex knew they had not meant him to wake up at all.

"You kept me asleep for six months? What about the wounds, the grenade, being shot several times."

"Yes," Courtney paused as if unsure how much he should let on but waved his hand in a submissive manner and sat on the bed. "I will tell you everything, but first," he paused for what seemed ages "are your hungry?"

"Not particularly Alex replied. Was I dead?"

"Let me tell you the facts first and then you can question me if you wish but I think it is you that has the answers."

Alex moved to the wall and sat on the floor opposite the old man, "You'll understand if I keep my back to the wall."

"Oh, we've made you into a cynic. Let me see if I can help you regain your faith in humanity. About eight months ago, on an archaeological dig, a luminous substance was discovered in a tomb in Cyprus. It seemed like gold dust at first but in very large quantities deep down in the earth. It was

48

supposed to be analysed and some of it was sent to one of our British scientists here in London. Anyone who came into contact with the substance developed, a virus which turned them into a brain eating monster. The virus was highly contagious and affected all those that were in the same vicinity as the carrier. The man at your bank reception, when we met, was one of the early varieties of this thing."

"Early varieties?" Alex shifted on the floor, his mind was racing, and he felt so alert, too alert.

"Yes, the early varieties were easily killed by a bullet or two to the head. As of late we have had to bombard them with all manner of weapons just to bring them down long enough to chop their heads off. Highly contagious, I was very lucky that night at the hotel, it did not come to close to me, however, it drooled onto you. Some of its saliva entered your mouth and I knew you were infected from the bite it gave you. I sent you to Depot five where the experiments use to take place."

"Use to?"

"The facility is shut down now, overrun, and the research there is not likely to be of any use to us." His face animated "you are the exception. You have not changed into a monster, you seem only to have taken its good points, the ability to heal."

"You said good points, is there more than one?"

Courtney looked twice his age, as though he were a miracle to be walking around. "We assumed that they were unintelligent, because they were monsters. It appears now that they are not only far advanced but also able to communicate with one another through telepathy. All the tests and such we were running rebounded back on us when we found out that they were learning more about us than we about them."

"You say them, but surely if it's a virus these people can be cured.?"

49

"Yes… if it's a virus. We just don't know. Which brings us to you, our only hope against these creatures? We have tried using your blood as a vaccine but to no avail. Of the thousands of others infected, it appears that only you have not turned."

"Oh, you mean like a werewolf, get bit become one, get drooled on become a brain eating thing. Hum, did you ever consider the fact that maybe it did not infect me?"

"Not really, I saw it happen, plus your intestines were hanging out from the grenade, we didn't put them back. You had ten bullets across your chest. We didn't remove them. You were taken for post mortem only to find that you were still alive and that new intestines had already begun to grow. It was as if your body was learning how to tend to itself. The damage from the bullets, all ten of them was nothing, as you had been shot before your body had healed you as soon as the bullets hit your body."

"How could you know that?" A realisation began to dawn on him.

"We have shot you over a hundred times since you have been here. We have also placed a grenade in your hand and watched as it went off only to see your hand untouched, as though your body already knew what was going to happen and had already made a new hand to seamlessly take its place. Your body not only cures itself but also absorbs the bullet, shrapnel or whatever into your system or just pops it out. It learns and develops antidotes," Courtney looked away in shame. "We have been poisoning you over the last few weeks with various things, each time you have remained alive and your body has found an antidote for everything. We tried to keep you under while all this was going on but now we have run out of sedatives that may have any effect."

"So you've been trying to kill me for six months, haven't been able to and now you need my help? You know there may be other people like me out there, only you may have killed them before they had a chance to develop. Do

50

you think that I can communicate telepathically with the other infected people?"

"Can you?"

Alex tried to look inside his mind and see if anyone else was there but it was just he and his distant memories looking back. He shook his head

"What happened to the girl?"

"She is alive and here in this complex."

"Which is where exactly?" His eyes glittered and Courtney was forced to answer him though he never realized it.

"London, deep down underneath Centre Point, the building is just a cover for this complex"

"That makes sense," Alex said and smiled warmly at Courtney. He really liked this man for some reason almost as if he was a relation.

"Will I be able to contact my ex-girlfriend to explain why I disappeared on her?"

"I'm afraid that won't be possible. There aren't many uninfected people left up there. We are under strict quarantine. We believe that Africa and maybe Europe have suffered the same fate. We have been talking to the Americans about a solution but I'm afraid there may be only one."

Alex stood up and walked over to Courtney. "You don't know if they are dead or not then? I want to find out."

"Yes, I thought that you might. As you are our last hope so to speak, we will give you our full co-operation. We have a mission for you to find out what is happening above us. We can no longer contact our over ground operatives and we fear that Centre Point is no longer under our control."

"Cassandra had a flat near here, in Charing Cross road just a few minutes walk."

"Really at this point you need to just go up to the top and re-establish communications."

"Yeah, right," Alex indicated the pyjama like outfit he was wearing.

"I'll have clothes brought straight to you," Courtney went to the door and paused. "You must come back after. We need your help."

"How can I refuse after all that you've done for me," Alex said with no intention of returning.

Alex was soon dressed and being led through the door of his cell along a well lit passageway. He had expected it to be lined by soldiers; they had dressed him in soldier's fatigues and supplied him with a bulletproof vest. Quite unnecessarily, he had been told by Courtney.

They reached an elevator and Courtney watched him enter.

"I can't go with you. Once you press the surface floor it will take you to the top. It takes about five minutes so don't be alarmed. This facility is the deepest one that has ever been created. Once outside, find the operations room and see what can be done to re-establish contact. Whatever else happens you need to make your way to the roof, there is a satellite dish there, about the size of a dustbin lid. It is extremely powerful but the node must point straight up for it to keep us in contact with the rest of the world. The lift will stop on the ground floor and then continue to the roof. Just be alert when the doors open. After you have been to the roof, return to the elevator and key in seven, nine, zero, Can you remember that?

"Seven, nine, zero, no problem. Not much of a code for such a secret place."

Courtney nodded and looked away. He moved into the elevator for a moment and laid his hand on Alex's shoulder.

"Samantha, the girl you met, is my daughter. If you are not back in one hour, she will be sent up to find you and that will be dangerous for her."

Alex stopped and looked into the old man's eyes, there was concern there "I'll be as quick as possible." He still had no intention of returning.

"Your daughter blew me up," he said a little more coldly than he meant to.

Alex watched as Courtney stepped out of the lift. He pushed the button, which had surface, written on it and the machine started to move upwards.

Alex had decided to go to his girlfriend's flat on Charing Cross road. The military could sort out its own satellite problems.

After what seemed an age the doors opened on the ground floor. Alex was wearing a high-level clearance identity badge, in case someone up here challenged him. There was no one around.

He left Centre Point and walked out into Charing Cross Road. He was stricken by changes before him.

Cars stood motionless parked in the middle of the road. A double decker sightseeing bus was sideways blocking part of the road. It looked like there were still people on board, he could see someone moving. He crossed over towards the bus; the driver was missing and the figure he had seen move had run up the stairs. It seemed small, maybe a child. He ventured nearer in an attempt to see some faces. There were about seven people still sitting on the bus, all with their back to him. They sat very still and he knew that they were dead. A face appeared at the window on the upper deck, a young girl

Alex jumped onto the bus and nearly fell over the tour guide strewn over the floor. His body was partially clothed, his trousers remained but his torso was naked and torn open. His hat lay beside his brainless head. Alex took a breath of fresh air from outside the bus. He looked down the aisle. There were people all over it and lying on the seats. The ones he had seen from the road had been propped up there. Something about them was strange. He suddenly realized that they were all wearing hats. He made his way across bodies to the first one and lifted the hat. The brain was missing. They had been propped up deliberately. It was a trap.

He heard the movement above him, a scurrying that must have belonged to the strange child he had seen. Had she set the trap, what had she become?"

He pulled the revolver out and made his way back over the bodies to the stairs.

"It's okay, you're safe now, come down," His voice sounded hollow and uncaring.

There was no reply.

Slowly with the gun poised he made his way up the stairs. He could have just left the bus, but he could not in case this was a real child. He half expected her to leap out at him, her teeth the size of an alligators, her face wild and mad with slime oozing down it.

He reached the top and looked around. The scene was worse up here. There was so much blood that some of it had not yet dried. There were also the bodies of soldiers piled on top of the other, their throats ripped out and their brains missing. He counted at least ten.

He heard crying towards the front of the bus, the girl was under a seat. He forced his way through the bodies to get to her, she sounded human.

"I won't hurt you" he said as he realized he had left the safety on the gun. He clicked it off and prepared to shoot.

He could see her now, her back against the far wall, a dead body at her side, dried blood on her face. Hers or someone else's, he thought.

"What's your name? He had a clear shot, he could have pulled the trigger without conversation but he was no soldier and he was not sure that this was anything but a child.

The girl stopped crying and looked at him abruptly, her eyes were swollen with tears and glassy as if she were trying to be far away. Her hands were clutching her dress in tight fists. He didn't sense that she was anything other than human and he believed his senses.

"I've come to help you," he put the gun in his pocket.

"They will get you," she said with staggered breaths.

"Uh huh, okay they don't seem to be here at the moment." He thought back to the trap downstairs and realized he was talking to the bait. As he looked up through the window he saw them walking towards the bus. There must have been fifty of them, they were surrounding the bus and yet they made no attempt to board it. The child threw herself at him and he nearly shot her on the spot but he realized that she was just trying to hug him.

"No, more," she said. "They told me to stay here, that I had to stay but they keep coming back and killing more."

"When was the last time someone came," Alex asked.

"I don't know, maybe a day ago or so. They decide which of them will eat and then that thing comes on the bus and kills!"

"Ssh, it's all right. How long have you been here?"

"I don't know maybe a few days," she looked up at him with red rimmed eyes, "they tried to make me eat but I wouldn't." The girl was thin, her cheeks pale.

"These creatures?" Alex asked.

"No, my parents, they tried to make me eat the meat and then when I wouldn't they brought me here and left."

Alex could feel the breeze through one of the broken windows; he drank the fresh air in and then stood up.

"What is your name?"

"Caroline, Caroline M…" She didn't want to say the last part to think of her parents.

"How old are you?"

"Just ten, it was my birthday last week."

Alex looked out of the window again there were more creatures out there now. They must have watched where he had come from as about fifteen of them were heading into Centre Point. Forty minutes had already passed, in another twenty Samantha would emerge from the lift into their midst.

The ones around the bus still stood there as though they were trying to decide something. One of them would point at him every now, he seemed something of an enigma to them.

"Why do they wait?" the girl asked

Just deciding who gets the dinner Alex thought. "They don't want us now. We can leave."

Caroline's eyes lit up for a moment, "we can go?"

"Sure, we'll just walk out," there's probably less than a hundred.

Alex hoped that with his immunity they could push through the creatures and run, if they timed it right they could get back to the lift just as Sam arrived, then they could go back to the bowels of the complex. Alex wondered if it might be better to kill the child. If she were immune also, they would experiment on her, if he even got her past the mob below.

"We need to wait another few minutes, just ten minutes to go."

The child shrugged and buried her head in his chest as one of the creatures boarded the bus and made its way upstairs.

Alex could hear it coming and placed his hand on the gun in his pocket. The creature had reached the top and glared at them from the stairwell with dark eyes moist from excitement.

This creature looked different to the one Alex had come into contact with before. It was somehow more advanced. Though the talons still remained, the body was more human in stature. It still wore the clothes of some unfortunate office worker it must have been before the change.

The face was contorted, the human qualities hidden behind a bloated forehead and greyish skin; there was no hair on its head and the nose just two slats in the skin. Almost reptilian but without scales, in fact, it looked slimy like a fish.

"Ahh, gremi," it made a sound that resembled nothing Alex had heard before, yet he was sure it was trying to talk.

"Hello," he replied "Nice day."

The creature took a step towards them. Alex pulled his gun and pointed it, the creature stopped.

"Why don't you just pretend this is your stop and get back off the bus'?

The creature's nostrils flared and sucked madly at the air, it looked confused but it seemed to know what a weapon was.

It looked at the child and she held her breath. The creature snorted and pointed at her then indicated himself.

Alex looked at his watch, it was time to go.

"Let's all get off the bus" he said.

The creature seemed to nod and a strange smile gripped its lips, as it backed down the stairs.

Alex followed holding on to the girl's hand behind him.

The creature leapt from the bus with a cat-like movement and communicated something to its friends.

Alex stepped off the bus, they were a few feet from him, crowding in, trying to get a look.

One of them stretched out a talon towards the girl and moved to take her. Alex rounded on him, "Back off!"

The creature obeyed, its head drooped as if in a bow and for the first time Alex thought that they might make it.

He moved forward and the creatures parted to allow him passage. He knew that Samantha would arrive any minute and he had to get to her before them.

He started to walk more quickly, they still parted before him, before he knew it, they were all behind him. He looked back, they were just watching him, he waved his hand towards the bus and they started to board it, he had no idea why, they just seem to be following his commands.

Alex entered Centre Point cautiously, there were creatures moving around in there but after a cursory glance they ignored him. Three of them were standing near the lift as the doors opened and Sam looked into their glassy eyes.

Alex dashed forward dragging the little girl with him, he cried out in some tongue he did not know, more like an animal noise and the creatures who had been about to devour Samantha stood back.

"Alex," Samantha held a grenade in her hand, she was about to pull the pin.

"It's all right," he moved forward and the creatures made way for him as the others had.

Samantha looked distrustfully at him and pulled the pin.

Alex leapt into the lift and grabbed the grenade; he threw it over the heads of the creatures towards the stairs then pushed Sam and Caroline into the lift. Sam looked into his eyes for a moment and punched in a series of numbers on the keypad. The door closed as the grenade went off but it blew the doors in. As they hit Alex they seemed to bounce off and the lift went down leaving a gaping hole at the top where the doors had been.

Chapter 6

The captain had continued to watch the nails grow on his former mate's hand as the horror grew and gnawed into his stomach. He had not been aware he was screaming until Larry had appeared by his side, anxiously undoing the restraints as he cast furtive glances at the emerging monster on the other bed.

Then the fear inside the captain's head began to disappear, he started to welcome a new feeling of power. His mind had become electrified, a thousand thoughts rushing through his brain at once and he was sure that they weren't his. Larry had succeeded in freeing him but suddenly fled, locking the cabin door behind him and by the sound of it blocking it with something large.

The captain looked at the other creature, it broke its restraints and grinned back at him. The face was discernible as his old colleague but in a rotten grotesque kind of way.

A hunger of the most intense kind filled the captain's stomach and he lunged off the bed towards the door. His eyes went temporarily blind and then they were back better than before. He could smell the people on the other side of the door, he could sense their fear and he knew Daniel was out there somewhere. The urge to kill him though had gone. It was as if new information had been fed into his brain, Daniel was important to them.

As the most advanced form yet, the captain would be their leader and would take on the name of Slayman, this notion crept into his brain and became truth.

A mirror was on the wall, which suddenly caught his attention. His reflection was not as he expected. He still retained his facial features, although his nails had grown to about six inches in length and had taken on a talon appearance. His hair remained in place, though his eyes were a little bloodshot. His legs continued to bend the right way and his mouth was not continuously drawling.

"We mean you no harm," he could speak!

61

He was as surprised on hearing the words leave his mouth as Larry was on the other side of the door.

"That's fine. You just wait till Daniel gets here, then we'll see," Larry nodded to Harry and Cynthia to move away from the barricades they had placed on the door.

"Let's seal off this corridor, I don't want to take any chances," Larry said.

"Larry, come quick!" It was Marshall's voice from the deck.

Larry rushed up there to find the whaling ship was bearing down on them. It was just anchoring itself, creatures could be seen moving on deck. The ship was only twenty feet away.

"Are they waiting for something?" Marshall asked as the creatures stood gazing at them across the small puddle of ocean that remained between them.

They were close enough to see into their blackened eyes and to see nothing human looking back. About twelve creatures looked down on them, but they made no move to get closer or board. They were waiting.

Larry crashed into Daniel's cabin and shook him until he woke, the cloth tearing on Daniel's shirt.

"What the hell is going on? What are these things?"

"I don't know," Daniel said as he his mind cleared. He had not been asleep, just resting and trying to think but it was almost as if he did not have complete control of his mind. A strange calmness had descended on him, he wasn't afraid, but he could see terror on the faces of those about him.

"They've caught up with us?" He knew it was a stupid question.

"Yes, they, they are just waiting," Larry replied.

"Daniel, what can we do?" Katrina asked her wide eyes brimming with tears which he longed to brushed away.

"We try to outrun them," Daniel said.

He swung his legs off the bed and retrieved his gun from his bag. No one seemed alarmed to see it now, in fact they looked positively pleased.

"Okay the plan is this. I go back on board, disable their ship, find some way to blow it up, meanwhile you get this boat moving as fast as possible. Don't wait for me."

"Daniel you'll be killed. Can't we communicate with them, see what they want?" Katrina asked.

"Communicate with them?" Daniel checked the gun was loaded.

"One of the men you brought aboard said they meant no harm," Larry said.

"One of the men?" Daniel felt his insides summersault within him. "The captain?"

"I don't know. One of them spoke to me through the door. He sounded friendly."

"Okay. Let's go talk to this friendly guy." Daniel felt the coolness of the gun in his hand and was ready.

They had to go on deck along to the old storeroom. The creatures still stood looking over from their ship. They had not been making a sound until they saw Daniel, then they started to scream. A high-pitched wailing noise that filled the sky. Katrina and Larry put their hands over their ears. Daniel could feel the sound boring into his head, "Shut up," he shouted and immediately the sound died.

"Okay, that was good," Daniel said to Larry who looked at him with a stranger's eyes.

"Jump over the side and drown!" Daniel shouted at them. They remained motionless on deck. "It was worth a try."

The door was still barricaded; Slayman and his mate had made no attempt to break free.

"Shame there's no window in the door to see what they're doing," Larry said.

"I'll tell you what they're doing. Thinking of ways to kill us." Daniel said.

"Daniel?" The voice was the captains but it was strange as though his mouth had changed shape.

Too many teeth for him to annunciate his words properly, Daniel thought.

"Daniel, I am called Slayman."

"Slay man? Oh great, like we're really going to want to have you running around."

"We want to be friends. You have seen things all wrong. I can explain them to you."

Slayman, the captain, leaned his head against the door and whispered, "We are in your service, Daniel."

Daniel jumped away from the door as if he had been burned.

"Did anyone else hear that whisper?"

Larry and Katrina shook their heads.

Daniel looked at the gun in his palm, it looked very small and inconsequential.

"I want you to get this boat moving. We'll see if they follow us. I need to take a look at what has happened to these guys. To be honest they were pretty nasty when they were human so I can't imagine they've got much worse. Block the passageway after you. If they get past me, I don't want them coming for you."

"Isn't there another way?"

"Not for now. I need to speak to this creature and see what it wants and why they haven't attacked us."

"I think we know why that is," Larry said as he gave Daniel a suspicious look and moved Katrina with him down the corridor. He looked back, "We'll start moving and see if they follow."

Daniel waited until they had left the corridor then he pulled the barricades away from the door. Larry had taken the key with him.

"Oh, the door is locked," Daniel called to the occupants on the other side.

"No problem," said Slayman and yanked it open.

Daniel held the gun up to Slayman's face as they looked at each other across the threshold. A smile played on Slayman's lips as he looked into Daniel's eyes.

"So we meet again so soon," Slayman hissed. His tongue seemed to have twisted in his mouth and he found it difficult to talk without lisping. He shook his head in the hope that his tongue would right itself.

"Sorry," he hissed again. "My tongue appears to be growing," a chuckle escaped through his throat.

Daniel was very close to pulling the trigger. He could see the captains face and yet the eyes and tongue were different. Then of course there were those razor sharp teeth with jagged edges. It looked as if he had enough for two people in his mouth.

Daniel took a step back as the other creature ambled up beside Slayman. It looked more alien, more bald and animal like, plus its legs bent the wrong way.

Slayman watched his eye movement from one to the other, "You see. I am different, the new breed and you are to be one of our governors."

"How are you different? Why?" Daniel asked keeping a wary eye on the other one which did not seem to have much self control as it drooled down its shirt.

"We evolve."

"Oh fine. How long before you become human?"

"We will surpass that," Slayman said with some disdain.

Daniel backed up a few more steps although he felt no fear, he knew that these creatures were not here to harm him. He could sense their thoughts, they were invading his brain telling him to join them and part of him answered, yes oh yes. He shook his head and put a hand up to his temple which throbbed.

"Mind games," he said.

"No, just the truth," replied Slayman.

"Why would anyone want to join with you?"

Slayman seemed to have regained control of his tongue it shrunk back into his mouth no longer popping out his cheek. "We are not yet as we will be. If you knew now how we will end up. You would beg to become a part of it."

Daniel felt some discomfort as his head continued to pound and the other creature moved towards him.

"Hungry," it said again and again, softly under its breath but to Daniel it may as well of shouted.

"Tell your friend to stop or I'll shoot it," Daniel said.

"No doubt you would my friend, but he must eat, he is hungry. Let him pass and seek out those which are of no use."

Daniel lifted the gun and fired into the belly of the advancing creature. He saw a momentary look of surprise on Slayman's face but it was soon replaced by that strange smile. The creature lunged for the gun and took more slugs in the side before it grabbed it and tossed it to the side as it pushed past Daniel and crashed through the door to the deck.

Voices still invaded Daniel's mind, they were desperate for him to accept them. He followed the creature up and then collapsed on the deck, his head weighed more than the ship. His vision had become blurry and the voices kept saying, join us.

A sharp blow hit him on the side of the head and he reeled back. He gazed up to see Slayman standing over him, its claw hand out stretched where it had struck him, his own blood on the tips of the talons.

"You may have to learn the hard way my friend," Slayman said.

Daniel awoke a little later. He realized that the boat wasn't moving. The other creatures had boarded from the whaler and stood around the small cluster of people in the middle of the deck where Slayman had gathered them. Katrina knelt at his side, Larry next to her. Sean, Jeff and Gary were all kneeling, Susan and Kieren stood with their arms around one another. Blood trickled into Daniel's eye, he felt for his pocket knife in his left boot.

"Which of these shall we dispose of first?" Slayman asked of his creature friends. "Which of these are food and which are useful, who should we keep and who to destroy?"

Daniel threw himself at Slayman and shoved the knife up to the hilt in his eye. Slayman screamed as the hot blood ran over his fingers. He pulled the knife out and threw it to the deck. The creatures stood around hollering and screaming but not knowing what else they should do.

Slayman fell to the ground and lay there twitching, Daniel stood up and addressed the creatures.

"Go back to your ship. I will come with you."

The humans around him were too scared to say anything, Katrina clung to his arm.

"You know what to do," he said to Larry.

"Come, we go back," Daniel was about to move when he saw Dennis and Louie come up from below. They had been attacked, part of one of Dennis's arms was missing, it just hung there in a bloody mess. Louie had no shirt and strips of his flesh were missing. They moved like the walking dead, already their eyes were dark, their teeth jagged and their lips pulled back in grimace.

Katrina screamed and then fainted at Daniel's side, Larry cradled her in his arms.

Daniel heard the voices in his brain, "Yes we go back," and with some relief he saw them all moving towards the other ship. They leapt effortlessly back up onto the deck like fine steeplechasers apart from Dennis who hit the side, tried to grab on with his bad arm and fell squealing into the sea. None of the others seemed to care. They carried Slayman's body, which unfortunately still breathed, with them.

Daniel followed them, he found the jump to the other ship was no problem for him, even though he was sure he would fall, it was too easy and he realized that he no longer was an ordinary human being.

On reaching the other ship Daniel gave orders to get underway. Some of the creatures were more intelligent than the others. They had no trouble understanding what he wanted. A scream brought his attention back to the deck, Katrina had been brought aboard. She was half dead with fright from the look of her as every part of her anatomy recoiled from the thing which held her.

"Who told you to bring her aboard, take her back!" He screamed at the creature which held her but it just hopped off on its strange legs to the captain's cabin below.

Daniel followed, he knew he would also find the dynamite there.

The creature put the girl on the bunk and left the cabin, it seemed to bow to Daniel as it left.

Daniel closed the door, he could see that they were moving away from the smaller boat though he did not know how long the creatures would obey him or when they would realize that he was not one of them. He realized that they could not read his thoughts the way he could understand theirs. Slayman had known, had looked into his mind and seen the truth, that he only wanted their destruction, he was not the one they sought. However, Slayman would have to convince them all of that before they would let him kill Daniel. Hopefully they were cannibalistic and would already have taken Slayman out of the picture.

He searched in the closet behind a secret panel which he had found previously on one of his snoops in the captain's cabin. There were guns, dynamite and plenty of ammo plus a nice machine gun which he thought would come in very handy.

Katrina moaned and opened her eyes, she looked at him and held out her hand for comfort.

Reluctantly Daniel replaced the weapons and took her hand. He sat next to her on the bed and held her until her tears stopped falling. How was he going to do this and get her off the ship alive?

"It doesn't matter about me," she said.

"Can everyone read my mind now?" Daniel groaned.

"I don't want to stop you from doing anything. How long are you going to wait until you attempt it?" Katrina asked glancing furtively at the door.

"I was going to wait half an hour and then blow the main engine compartment. I figure it will take the other boat an hour to get back and find us. But now…."

"You must still wait. If we are not far enough away from the other ship they may just transfer back to it."

"Well, I'm hoping the dynamite will get them, but then, who knows."

"Be with me for a while," she said softly. "I never really knew who you were, I wanted to know you so much."

He lay down and put his arms around her. He was about to speak when she kissed him and for a moment he could imagine that they were on cruise in the Mediterranean, maybe on a honeymoon. He pushed her away gently but she clung on, her fear spilling into her desire, stripping away her inhibitions so that she wanted only him.

"Shut the world out for me, Daniel."

He kissed her hard then and knew that he could not refuse her a means of escape, he did not want to refuse her. There were horrific creatures wandering above them on deck, a madman who might still be alive and hungry for his blood and with ease his mind blocked it all out. Only Katrina and he existed, only they were alive in the world and perhaps he would kill them both with the gun after he had set the dynamite. And so they lay for over an hour holding each other, their minds refusing to accept reality.

Chapter 7

Two days had passed since their return to the underground fortress. Alex had been returned to his cell and had had little contact with anyone. He had asked many times about the little girl but had had no reply from the soldiers who brought him his food. It made him angry that somewhere in this complex they were probably doing experiments on her, maybe even hurting her to see how she recovered. They would constantly be taking blood samples and putting her through more pain. He decided that if they did not explain to him today, he would break out and free her. The iron door no longer looked that tough. He felt stronger than ever, a change had come over his mind also, it felt serene as if nothing could hurt him or those he protected, and he wanted to protect the child.

His thoughts were interrupted by the cell door opening. Samantha stood in the doorway, her hair loose on her shoulders, her normal business or army fatigues replaced by a plain but alluring dress. It was the first time he had really noticed her face and she was beautiful.

"Another test?" He asked attempting a smile. The anger flared in him, it now had a focus, Sam. She had been trying to kill him since he'd met her.

"I thought that it was time to tell you what is happening. What has been happening in the past few days," she shifted uneasily under his gaze her eyes refusing to meet his.

"Take a seat," he replied trying to keep the hostility from showing in his voice. "It seems I don't warrant an extra chair."

He didn't want to sit on the bed, it made him vulnerable, so he decided to sit on the floor opposite Samantha, he could also keep his back against the wall that way. She looked even more uneasy.

"I could ask for another chair," she offered.

"No don't bother. They must be in short supply and I'm very comfortable on the floor, after all, animals have to stay off the furniture."

"Look, I'm terribly sorry about all this. You are probably very angry and you have a right to be. I could have killed you up there."

"No, you couldn't," Alex said with some satisfaction.

"I could have hurt Caroline and I realize now that you were trying to protect her."

"And you," Alex said dryly leaning his head against the wall.

"And me. I just thought that you had turned, they weren't attacking you, they were responding, some sort of communication between you had me confused. Plus you didn't throw the grenade at them but over their heads as if you didn't want to hurt them." Samantha found this extremely difficult. She had an overwhelming attraction towards this man, yet she didn't know if that came from her or if there was something biological within him from the virus which had made her feel that way. She wondered how she would have felt if they had met before any of this happened and then pushed the thought away. She may have to kill him someday, maybe soon, maybe as soon as they found a way to kill him.

"When can I see Caroline?" Alex asked. He looked directly into her eyes, she looked away.

"She is well, you can see her anytime you like. I'm a little surprised you haven't gone looking for her. We wondered how long you would remain here sulking."

"Remain here sulking! You want me to break out?"

"The door wasn't locked, it hasn't been since you regained consciousness and we realized that you really are on our side. For now anyway."

Alex laughed, he couldn't stop, the door hadn't been locked, he should have tried it.

"I just assumed," he stopped. "What do you mean I was unconscious? How long?"

"You were out for a couple of days, during that time you were delirious. You seemed scared to death. You told us everything that had happened outside and how frightened you were."

"I didn't feel like that at the time," Alex felt angry again. She had seen him in a fit of fear, known what the human side of him was like. Found out that he wasn't so special after all.

"We think that fear is stored within you so that when you are in a dangerous situation you are very calm. Afterwards, when you feel safe, your body shuts down and is consumed with the fear it should have felt earlier. We thought you might die of fright but obviously you did not."

"Any idea why Caroline and I are immune to infection," Alex stood up and started to pace his cell.

Samantha felt very disconcerted by this movement, she tried to keep her gaze on him but every time he looked her way she had to break off.

"You aren't immune. Caroline may be. But you are definitely infected; it has done some amazing things to you, unless you were superman before."

He stopped pacing in front of her, she immediately stood up she couldn't have him looking down on her it gave him the edge. Standing up caused her to be closer to him than she realized, they were barely a foot apart.

Alex wanted to reach out to her, to kiss and hold her and far more, he turned away quickly. His feelings were too strong, he was sure that the virus was affecting him, he should hate her. He moved further away and turned back, she had a questioning look on her face and he made himself a promise that he would never become involved with this woman. Besides if he had tried to kiss her someone would surely have jumped out of somewhere and shot him. He expected that this was a side effect, intense attraction to beautiful women. Next time he met one, his theory would prove itself he thought.

"What's the matter Alex?"

He liked the way his name sounded on her lips.

"I'd like to see Caroline now. Make sure you people haven't stuck some pins in her or something." That was it, he thought, keep the hostility up between them Remember what she was part of and how they had treated to him.

Samantha looked hurt for a moment and he wanted to rush over to her and explain that he trusted her. But I don't he reminded himself, she hates me.

"I'll take you to her now. I hope you don't think that I would be a party to the torture of a child?"

"No. Just the torture of a grown man, maybe more." He thought she might slap him, her eyes narrowed but she kept her cool and he was disappointed. He would have welcomed the slap. Any contact with her would have been a sweet interlude, to feel her hand on his face. He shook his head and followed her out of the room; he would have followed her anywhere. I've got to get out more, he thought.

They passed through a long door made of bars which had to be opened from the other side. Samantha cast a wary look towards Alex, he showed no reaction to this extra security. They walked on until they could see a large steel door at the end of the corridor, there were six guards in the area and two on either side of the door.

"Just precautionary," Samantha said with a wan smile. Alex gave no reaction.

In fact Alex was very alarmed and angry but he decided to keep his emotions as masked as possible. As the turbulence of feelings welled inside him, he made sure that nothing reached his face. He had the feeling that if he did show anything, Samantha would just refuse to take him any further and he was not ready for her to stop co-operating with him yet. First he wanted to see how Caroline was and whether they should remain here. After all, the creatures on the outside had not seemed harmful to him or those he protected.

They reached the door and Samantha punched a few numbers into a keypad on the right hand side. One of the soldiers smiled at her but she didn't smile back. Alex wondered if she would have done if he hadn't been standing next to her. The soldier, Alan Marsh it said on this uniform, had obviously wanted to say something to her but had thought better of it.

The door opened and they entered a room very different to the one they had just left. There were two beds along the far corner of the wall and another door led off into a play area where they could see Caroline through a glass window. She had two scientist types with her, showing her various things, asking her questions and wearing some sort of contagion suits.

"I'm sure that makes her feel at ease," Alex said as he went effortlessly forward through the locked door into the sealed area.

"Alex!" Caroline had seen him and ran into his arms as if he was her natural family and had been with her always.

She glanced back at the men in contagion suits and then at Samantha.

"How are you Caroline?" Alex asked as she released him and he saw the tears in her aged eyes.

"I'm okay. I wondered why you didn't come, but they said you were sick and then these men in strange outfits kept coming to ask me questions. Do they think I'm sick as well?"

"No, those men are just being extra careful. We gave you an all clear yesterday didn't we? You see me walking around outside now don't you?" Samantha felt Alex's gaze on her face.

"You were in here with her?" Alex asked.

"Yes, I had to be quarantined also. Just in case I was too close to one of those things upstairs. We know that you can't pass it on, we've done every kind of test on that theory," She looked away and Alex felt very uncomfortable.

"Every sort of test?"

"I'll explain it another time," she glanced at Caroline.

"I don't even want to know." He squeezed Caroline's hand.

"I'm hungry," Caroline said.

Alex felt a short intake of breath from Samantha. They really hate to part with their food rations, he thought.

"Okay, get the door open, we are going to find the canteen and have a proper meal."

"I don't know if we're ready to do that," Samantha began.

Alex brushed past her and put his hand on the door handle to the main hall, it was locked. He glanced back at Samantha, she shook her head.

He placed his hands on either side of the door and yanked it open. It took considerably less out of him than he expected. The locking mechanism had snapped off inside.

"Wow that was cool," Caroline said her face lighting up for the first time since they had met.

"I was hoping you wouldn't notice," Alex said,

"The door is halfway off its hinges," Samantha said with considerable restraint. How could she not notice?

Eight guns were pointed at them as they moved through the door away.

"Stand down," Samantha yelled moving herself in front of the others. "The quarantine has been declared as over and we are going to the mess hall." She had a calm dominance about her, the men complied immediately with her wishes.

79

"Shall we follow you ma'am?" Asked Alan Marsh.

"Why, don't you know the way?" Alex asked as he sauntered by with Caroline. They stopped at the end of the hall.

"You won't find it without me." Samantha said something to Alan Marsh who nodded and appeared to stand down.

"We'll wait for Samantha," Alex said to Caroline with a tight smile.

Samantha overtook them and beckoned for them to follow her and the eight soldiers followed at a distance.

Caroline chatted freely as they walked along; she talked about things that happened in her old life before her parents changed. About her pet dog, Spike, named after an adversary of Buffy the Vampire Hunter and about numerous friends she had at school.

The mess hall was empty when they got there, apart from one wary looking cook behind the counter.

They all took a tray and moved along the counter.

"Could I have some cereal please?" Caroline asked.

"Sure," the man scurried away out the back. He returned with a packet of frosted cereal and a jug of rice milk.

"I'll have some toast, a couple of eggs and mushrooms." Samantha said.

"No eggs," the cook said without sympathy.

"Just toast then."

"Just coffee and toast for me," Alex said aware of the tension building in the mess hall.

They all sat down to eat at one of the long tables, the soldiers watched from the doorway.

Samantha watched them eat, they seemed so natural just like a father and daughter on a normal day not surrounded by death and a number of soldiers waiting to blow their brains out if they did anything out of the ordinary.

"You are a vegetarian." Samantha said suddenly.

"Sure, you got me. I see you finally found out my secret," Alex smiled.

"I'm a vegetarian as well," Caroline cried out with glee, glad to have something in common with her hero.

"So am I," Samantha said. "In fact so is everybody on this base now. We established that there was no sign in your stomach of any meat remnants sometime ago. Meat stays in the system for around five years. Since then certain experiments have shown us that vegetarians are immune to being turned. But they don't develop your gifts. We need to know more about you, I'd like to spend more time with you, learn about your life, the background that's not in your file, things that could have happened to you to make you so different."

Alex shrugged, "Sure I don't have any objection to spending more time with you as long as you promise not to try and kill me, again."

"I promise I won't try and kill you. I never was part of that, I hope you can believe me. I'm not a scientist, I am....'Samantha's voice died away as she realized that she had tried to kill him twice and probably would be again.

Chapter 8

Daniel dreamt he was on a barren land standing at the top of a hill. There were several creatures roaming the terrain below him. They all looked perfectly normal, perfectly human but Daniel knew they were not. Another man stood at his side, one he had not yet met. The other man was about the same age and of similar height, he was carrying a machete and a radio.

"Can we save any?" the other man asked.

"No," Daniel replied, "These lands are dead to us, no more human life exists here."

"I'll call it in then," the other man said and spoke into the radio, "This is Cartier, we are declaring a dead land."

The next moment the sky was filled with a vague humming sound which grew into a loud roar and then a soft whistling. A missile plummeted from the sky. A nuclear one which hit the wasteland below and turned it into a colourful ball of fire. The mushroom cloud rose high above them as they stood there mourning mankind. Daniel felt the other man's hand on his shoulder, as they shared despair, he looked down at it and saw talons gripping his flesh so hard that blood spilled onto the ground. He turned quickly and saw Cartier's face, normal and yet the eyes shone too bright, then he smiled and the teeth began to grow.

Daniel woke up with a start. He didn't know how long he had slept or how. Katrina slept still, her breathing intermingled with short yelps and moans. Daniel decided not to wake her, whatever she was dreaming about could not be worse than being awake.

He put his boots on, picked up the dynamite and hid it in his coat then he left Katrina and made his way towards the engine room.

He saw few creatures along the way, the ones he did just bowed and moved away. It made him wonder if he should be blowing them up, perhaps he should actually be trying to communicate with them. The ship was just drifting, there was no sign of the smaller vessel from the deck. It occurred to him that these creatures must be very hungry. What were they going to eat in the absence of humans? Perhaps he might get them to do some fishing, learn to make fish their main diet, not kill them in a flurry of fire.

No, he had to kill them, he told himself and was unsure if the feelings of compassion were his or being channelled to him from the monsters themselves.

One of them gazed at him as he walked by, it was definitely looking at him in awe and they were all looking far more human. He wondered if maybe they had some sort of virus which after running its course and turning them into brain-eating monsters would turn them back into the people they once were and they would go on with their lives unaware of any of the bloody crimes they had committed. He would still blow them up though. He could not afford to think they could be cured, for if they spread, he knew from his nightmare that they would dominate the world.

He went through the galley and saw five of them eating a normal meal of omelette and chips, one of them stood where the chef used to and cooked things. They gazed at him as he passed by.

"Just taking a walk around the ship," he said. He was sure they nodded. Perhaps he wasn't seeing them as they truly were, they could have put him under some sort of hallucinatory spell but he didn't think that was very likely.

"Can you all swim?" He asked suddenly surprising himself.

They looked back blankly and he could hear their thoughts race through him. "Why would he ask us that? Does he not know us, is he not the one?"

"No problem, just curious." He hurried away and resigned himself not to speak to them again. Still they had been eating ordinary food and if you ignored the fact that they still had those horribly pointed teeth and the long taloned nails the rest of their body seemed to have returned to its normal shape.

He made it to the engine room; no one was there and he started to place the plastic explosive. He knew about timers, priming and the best places to do the most damage on a ship from his anti-terrorist training with the FBI.

Three creatures ambled in as he finished placing the last bit but he hadn't set the timers yet.

The creatures looked at him and bowed and proceeded to get the engines running. He felt his mind probing theirs and received a response that they were heading inland. They looked startled for a moment, they had felt his mind inside theirs and yet they couldn't get into his. They continued their work without looking at him again.

He was wondering what his next move should be when a foghorn gained his attention, another ship was close buy.

Hurriedly he made his way to the top deck and saw a British navy frigate bearing down on them. On deck the creatures all stood around with their taloned hands behind their back and their mouths closed, this way they looked normal apart from their tattered clothing.

The ship was close, a voice sounded over a speaker.

"Ahoy there. Are you in difficulty?" The voice had a clipped English accent.

Daniel moved forward, the creatures expected him to speak for them, to protect them.

Daniel rushed to the radio and spoke back to the ship, "I need to come aboard."

The creatures passed small glances between them and so many unspoken words that Daniel could not get it all.

"I'll be bringing a woman with me." Daniel said.

"We'll send a launch for you," the captain said.

Daniel wondered how much the navy commander knew about what was on this ship and if he did know, why was he risking contamination by allowing access to his ship? Daniel had assumed that the Cafistan had managed to get some help. He rushed down to the cabin and woke Katrina, he half carried her back up the stairs. None of the creatures tried to stop him. They just sent waves of confusion in his direction.

A launch had drawn up against the ship; two heavily armed men were aboard, they wore contamination suits.

"Climb down Katrina, I'm right behind you," Daniel said as the creatures closed on their position.

A monster started to climb down after Daniel, he felt that it had been told to guard him. He jumped to the launch and told them to go, they left immediately and the creature gave out a howl of disappointment.

"It had been chosen to protect me," Daniel thought to himself. Its name was Murphy.

The launch sped back to the ship with some speed, the sailors kept their guns trained on Daniel and Katrina the whole time. When they reached the ship they were helped aboard by men wearing contamination suits.

"Just being cautious," the captain said as he emerged from nearby. "Are you Daniel Mason?"

"Yes, how did you know?"

"We ran into the Greenpeace boat, they told us this fabulous story of monsters and how they abducted the two of you. We didn't know what to expect, perhaps some chemical warfare, drugs."

"But you still took it seriously," Daniel said.

"We take everything seriously in the navy sir," the captain said.

"Good, then you'll take this seriously. I've planted some plastic explosive in their engine room. All you need to do is fire on the ship and set the explosives off." Daniel took his badge from his back secret pocket and flashed it at the captain.

"I know what I say might seem very odd, but I can assure you that these things are very dangerous. The virus doesn't seem to affect vegetarians in the same way."

"You're a vegetarian are you?" The captain asked.

"Yes but that has nothing to do with it." Daniel did not need special powers to know what was going through Captain Random's mind.

"So you want me to blow up a whaling ship and you just happen to be a vegetarian who is also a member of a fringe of activists who have been known to resort to acts of terrorism?"

"I am not a member of the fringe, I was just undercover and I can tell you that they are not terrorists. They would not want to blow the ship up," Daniel knew he was losing the battle. "If not then I need to go back."

"I think you had better spend some time with us Mr Cartier while we investigate who you are to start with. We've been having trouble with our communications but as soon as we're back on line, we will find out more about you. Show this couple to a spare cabin and put a guard on the door." Captain Random turned away.

"If you want to observe, do it from here!" Daniel shouted.

"Don't worry," Captain Random said over his shoulder, "we won't be taking any risk of infection."

Daniel found himself once more in a strange cabin with a guard outside the door, though this one was a lot nicer. He could see the other ship from the porthole. Katrina had fallen asleep on one of the bunks, she looked awful and he was afraid that she somehow been affected by the virus. He watched her for a while, her skin was very pale, he felt the urge to check her teeth but decided against it. Her fingers still looked normal.

A noise outside drew his attention to the porthole, a launch was making its way towards the other ship. Fine, he thought, find out for yourselves. He felt weary and lost, for all he knew they were on their way to disarm his explosive. Perhaps he should have mentioned that they'd probably be eaten as soon as they stepped aboard. The launch had almost reached the other ship. He watched it pull up and could just make out four figures climbing aboard. Suddenly there were voices in his head. A hundred questions came at him so fast, he struggled for breath. "Can we eat these? What do they want? Where are you? Why have you not returned?"

The silent voices were deafening. He tried to shut them out. Then he tried to send a reply. *Don't eat them. Tell them to return to their ship.* He knew somehow that they couldn't hear him. It seemed his affinity with them was one way. He needed to be within earshot for them to hear his voice, he could not save the sailors. The voices in his mind ceased and he was filled with a new sensation. The satisfaction of a craving, the creatures were eating.

Daniel banged on the door calling for the captain and eventually the guard went to fetch him. Daniel kept looking out the porthole but he couldn't see anything of the men, he knew they were dead anyway. Worse, he knew how they had died and that they had still been alive as the brain juice was sucked from their bodies.

The captain entered the cabin, the guard close behind.

"I have been told that you had to see me, you have become quite agitated and I presume it is because of the launch I sent to the other ship."

"You sent them to disarm the explosive."

"Yes, and to have a look around."

"They won't be coming back, and the explosives are still intact," Daniel said, trying to stop the contempt from showing in his voice. It didn't work.

"But they are coming back, as we speak," the captain pointed towards the porthole. The launch was making his return.

"No, they're not on it. Quick contact them, check who's there, they're monsters."

The guard pulled his weapon and held it on Daniel.

"You do seem to be getting rather upset. I think you should try to calm down. That girl should go to sick bay anyway," the captain said as he turned to leave.

"Wait. Look. On the off chance that I'm not as crazy as a loon, don't leave us in here. Let us be on deck so that we can make sure nothing happens when they get here."

The captain sighed heavily, his patience had all but run out, he called another sailor in and had him carry Katrina to sick bay.

"Let me stay with her?" Daniel asked. He was pretty sure that if he said he could communicate with these creatures they would throw him in the brig. Though strictly speaking, it was them that communicated with him.

Captain Random was a good man, he could tell there was a lot of fear in this young man and that he had been through a great deal. He thought that it might do Daniel good to see the other men arrive, perhaps once he saw that they were not dead, he would feel better and this strange fantasy he had weaved for himself would evaporate.

"Okay, Daniel, let's go and watch them come aboard."

Daniel noted that he was suddenly being called by his first name and assumed that the captain was humouring him. That was fine as long as he got a chance to stop the creatures from getting on board; unfortunately they were already standing on deck when the captain and he reached there.

They looked like four ordinary men from a distance but once you were close enough to see the differences, claws, teeth, eyes it was probably too late.

Random stood dumbfounded at Daniel's side. The sailors nearest where the creatures had come aboard were in alert position. It was obvious from their ragged clothes beneath the plastic suits they had taken from the sailors that they were not navy.

Still, they stood and waited, there was blood and stains down their shirts, their eyes darted to the twenty or so men with guns trained on them.

As soon as they saw Daniel they tried to move forward to get to him.

"My name is captain Random. Stop your advance or I will have you shot," Captain Random said.

They continued to move forward, their movement awkward as their knee joints seemed to move in both directions. The sailors opened fire without much effect at first. After twenty or so bullets had been pumped into each victim, they fell to the ground, the last reaching out his taloned hand in a beseeching manner to Daniel, his words dying in Daniel's brain, "help us."

Sailors were already running over to the bodies, checking they were dead, examining what sort of creatures they were.

Daniel watched in horror as blood from the creature's glared red on the sailor's hands. "Don't touch them, we don't know how they pass the virus!"

Unseen the blood disappeared into the skin of the people handling the bodies.

"Where did these creatures come from?" Random asked.

"They're infected humans, they're people just like you and me." Daniel thought of Slayman, he had been evil to start with, they certainly weren't like him. "They were people, anyway," he corrected.

"Put the bodies down below," Random ordered.

"No," Daniel said, "Throw them over and blow up the ship, they'll send more."

"How do you know so much about what they'll do?" Random asked, his lips forming a slight scowl.

"I hear them in my head. They want me to do something for them. I can read their thoughts but they can't read mine. To communicate with them I have to speak out loud, that's the only way they can hear me, even so they might not take any notice."

"What are they thinking now then?" Random asked carefully.

Daniel felt he was still being humoured but he tried to concentrate on the recess in the back of his mind where the voices were, it was silent.

"I don't know at the moment, maybe they are too far away," they were saying they were coming, that everyone on board his ship would die, that Random would die last, painfully, horribly without mercy. Daniel didn't know how much to pass on, what good it would do.

"Too far away," Random shrugged a small contemptuous smile.

"All right, I can hear them speak your name. They know you now, they learn from each other. What happens to one creature is a lesson to all of them. They are coming and we have to kill them first."

"Come with me," Random led Daniel to his office, he issued some orders to his men, and then they went inside and closed the door.

"Would you like a drink Daniel?"

The change of tact threw Daniel for a moment; he went to the porthole and looked towards the other ship.

"Don't worry we are on full alert. If any of them should try to get to us, we will take action." Random poured himself a drink and sat down in the big chair behind an ornate wooden desk. "Now I need to ask you some questions and find out exactly what you think we're dealing with here."

"What I think we're dealing with," Daniel snorted disdain.

"Okay, you have your own view on things; I am just a ship's captain who has happened along. Until I check out who you are, I can't establish whether you are in your right mind, is that a fair assessment?"

Daniel sank down into a chair opposite.

"Look why don't you call me Ben, you're not in the navy after all. I want you to feel at ease. You've obviously been through a lot and we need to talk about the way forward. You must realize I can't just blow up a ship without authority from the navy. At this moment we still have no communications."

"Captain, doesn't the fact that you have no communications alert you to the possibility that this is more than a threat here. This could be all over the world."

"What could?"

Daniel was perplexed to the point of grabbing Ben and shaking him but he restrained himself, though he suspected his impatience was more than obvious in his eyes.

"I'll take that drink, bourbon no ice," Daniel wandered over to the porthole again.

"Scotch okay?"

"Sure, why not."

Ben offered Daniel the drink and indicted taking a seat again. Daniel rolled his eyes and sat down.

"Why don't you tell me how it started?" Random was persistent.

"Here we are having a nice drink and a chat while they prepare to kill everyone on board." Daniel almost laughed.

"Why would they want to kill everyone? Why didn't they kill you before if they are so hostile and where did they come from?"

Daniel tried to think back. Where had they come from? Who was the first to become one of them?

"It started with a man called Buda, I think. I didn't see it I was unconscious at the time but Slayman told me about it."

"Slayman?" Ben asked

"He's one of them, dead now, I think," but no he was not dead, that same evil presence was still on board the other ship. He was waiting.

"Buda was a small guy, he did the whaling for the money to pay for his daughter's education in Egypt. He would take any odd jobs he could find, a man of many different facets. He told me he had even worked on an archaeological dig just before joining the ship. Perhaps he had volunteered for some experiment that had gone wrong and this is the result, he was the only one I could feel anything but revulsion for. At least he had a good reason for being a criminal though not an excuse. He talked a lot about her, she lives in England, her name is...... Marcia or Marsupial, I don't know."

"A germ warfare type thing?" This was something Ben could understand. "Perpetrated by whom, which country?"

"I don't know, I'm just turning the facts over out loud. Perhaps something from another planet landed and zapped him with a ray gun. How the hell am I supposed to know? We don't even know if he was the first one on board to go down, we only have what Slayman told me."

"What is this affinity you have with the creatures?" Ben asked the question he most wanted to.

"I don't know, I really wish I did."

Their attention was taken by shots fired on deck, Ben grabbed his pistol from the drawer but they found that the cabin door would not open.

"Let me try it!" Daniel yanked at the handle, it came off in his hand. He threw himself against it and knocked it the other way. He punched a hole through it, they could see a metal bar was jamming it. The shots continued on deck, then they heard the launch leaving. Daniel knocked the bar out of the way and they raced up on deck.

Ten broken bodies lay strew about on the deck. The launch was halfway across to the other ship.

"What's going on?" Ben shouted.

"We were taken by surprise, our own men. They turned into something else and just pushed people out of their path. Three of them made it to the launch with the girl," a man answered, there was blood on his arms and head. Daniel wondered if he would turn.

"The girl? Katrina's on that boat?" Daniel could hear the voices in his brain. "Now you will return to us. Now you will lead us, or," there was a pause, then the voices almost sang together, "or not and she will die.

"Fire on that launch, don't let it reach the ship," Ben shouted.

"No! You can't do that! what about Katrina?"

Ben looked at him with a hostile glare but he rescinded the order to fire.

"What do they want her for?" Ben asked.

"I don't know. But I have to go back there to find out. Once I'm there, give me five minutes to get her over the side and then blow it up, can you do that?"

Ben looked around at the dead and wounded about him plus strange bodies of men he had known that had become alien to him.

"Don't touch any of the dead! Everyone immediately wash your hands and if you have been in contact with any enemy creature, report to the brig to await further instructions, you must be quarantined."

"Vegetarians won't be affected," Daniel offered.

"All vegetarians report to my office immediately," the captain said over the tannoy.

The launch had reached the other ship.

Daniel looked towards it. "I'm so sorry Katrina" he kept repeating. He knew the captain was not going to let him go to get her. They were waiting, he could feel them, though the voices were silent, they knew he would come.

Ben nodded as Daniel dived into the water and saw a sad resolution in Ben's eyes. He started to swim as fast as he could towards the other ship. He knew he would not have the five minutes he had asked for.

Chapter 9

Alex waited in the underground board room for the others to show up. He was included in a lot of things now, they had accepted him as an ally who would not betray them, or so he chose to believe.

Samantha would be here any moment, he subconsciously smoothed his hair into place and felt his throat constrict slightly. He could not deny that she held a great attraction for him. It was difficult to be with her and not give any sign of the way he felt, but he knew that this was the way it had to be. He didn't think that she had noticed, if she had there had been no sign of any interest from her and for this he was grateful.

He paced around the room becoming irritated. Why was it always him that was left waiting for them?

Since the vegetarian discovery there had been much excitement in the complex, for the first time they had something to work with. Experiments had begun almost immediately though Alex had been unaware of these. With over two hundred people in the complex, they managed to find five vegetarian volunteers. The results had been depressing. They had just decided that vegetarians were immune when four of their test subjects went down. It turned out that the subject had to have had no meat of any kind in their diet for a number of years, at least five. The one who remained unaffected gained no extra powers but was still under observation. Her name was Sergeant Carla Wilkins. She had been in the army most of her life and had ended up here over a year ago when she won a transfer and a promotion. Her speciality was combat, she had guarded many an important guest, had fought in more than one war, sometimes under cover and had no problem with following any kind of orders. In fact, she lived for orders, they gave meaning to her life and somewhere along the way she had managed to lose the ability to make her own decision on things that really mattered. When they had asked for volunteers of the vegetarian kind, she had been the first to raise her hand even though she hated not eating meat. She had craved it every day for the last ten years, since she gave it up. The last piece of meat she had eaten had not been an animal and the nightmare of that event still haunted her.

Something was still different about Alex. It was finally discovered that he had an allergy to meat and a rare element in his blood that they couldn't identify. It was unknown as to whether the element had always been there or if that was caused by the virus. They had run more tests on him.

He sat down on the comfortable chair with his back to the wall waiting for their arrival. He wondered where Caroline was today.

Samantha walked in smiling, something she did rarely.

"I see you have the comfy chair again," she said.

"Those who arrive first, on time for a meeting, get the best position," Alex responded.

Samantha walked over to him sat on his lap unexpectedly, her fingers traced his mouth.

"I expect you know a lot about the best position," she said and kissed him.

His arms involuntarily moved around her as he pulled the kiss deeper into his body. She shifted on his body and he kissed down her neck opening the blouse with his fingers as she put her head back and sighed.

She nipped his ear, "I love you", she said and slipped her hand under his shirt

"I love you too," he responded.

"Alex? Wake up," Samantha's voice far away.

"Alex", a man's voice.

Alex woke up with a start almost falling out of the chair, he had been waiting for over an hour. Samantha stood looking at him quizzically.

"What were you dreaming about?" She asked, a half smile on her lips.

"Nothing," he said as realisation dawned.

"Must have been something. You were talking and you're all flushed", Samantha pushed him further. She tried to take his pulse but he withdrew his hand quickly.

"Nothing. I was dreaming about something, does it matter?"

"It might", an older man, Major Reeves said. "Your subconscious could be trying to tell us something of use".

"No, it was nothing", Alex shook his head.

"Perhaps we should have the medical team put him under, try hypnosis if he can't remember what it was", Samantha continued.

"Hey, I'm in the room. I really hate it when you just forget or ignore me and discuss what is going to happen to me as if I'm just a pet".

"You seem agitated," Samantha shrugged. "more so than usual", she added.

"What does that mean, more so than usual?" Is that how they saw him an agitated experimental subject?

"We need to know what you dreamt that wound you up like this. You're normally calm and collected", the major said.

"She just said I was agitated," Alex said petulantly.

"I didn't mean, look just tell us the dream okay", Samantha clicked on her small recording machine she always carried and put it in front of his mouth.

Alex shrugged. "Fine. I was walking in the park when a bird landed on me", he wondered if it sounded like he was making it up.

"What sort of bird was it?" the major asked.

"Which park?"

"I don't know, sparrow perhaps. Anyway, um, a dog walked by and the sparrow turned into a polar bear and they danced off into the sunset."

The major and Samantha gave each other a meaningful glance.

"So why did you say I love you?" Samantha asked.

"I did?" Alex expelled a huge sigh of agitation and quickly checked himself. He didn't want them locking him up again.

"I love polar bears, they've always been a favourite creature of mine I guess."

"Well okay. Did the bear say it loved you first?" Samantha asked.

"No, why?," Alex asked hesitantly.

"Well, you said I love you too. One would think that the bear must have said it first?"

Alex was perplexed, "Maybe it did. I don't remember." He wished the ground would swallow him up. His face was burning.

"I'll get on it right away", the major said and left the room.

"Get on what?" Alex asked as the older man left the room.

"Well its been decided that you are a very important person and that everything you do or say is of interest. Your dreams in particular could hold the clue to our salvation." Samantha tossed her hair back and smiled at him. It was obvious she didn't think that the world revolved around him or that he was their only salvation.

"It was just a dream" he said a little stunned.

"Even so, I expect the Major is on his way to find out how we could get a polar bear in here. Probably putting a team together now to check out the zoo in Regent's Park, see if the animals are still alive, capture a polar bear, transport it back here past all the monsters and see if it holds the key." Her eyes flashed a little at the end. She was angry and he knew that she didn't believe his dream.

"He's not really going to." He paused, her eyes were hard and her fingers were drumming on her crossed arms.

"Do you want to come clean now or wait until you're leading Operation Bear? You know you would have to go with them to control the creatures."

Alex shook his head and wondered how he had got himself into this.

"Okay." He said softly. "I was dreaming about a girl."

Samantha picked up the phone called through to the major.

"Sir, its Samantha. His dream was about a woman. Yes sir I'll wait with him."

Alex started to laugh, he couldn't stop, the more he thought about the bear the more he laughed. His laughter was cut short when he caught sight of Samantha's face from the corner of his eye.

"Sorry," he mumbled.

The major walked back in and threw his briefcase on the desk.

"What the hell are you playing at? You're the only lead we have, our only hope of finding our way out of this and you're playing games with us?"

Alex felt chastised as if he had been a kid caught playing hooky from school.

"Sorry," he said and sat up at the table.

Samantha and the major sat down and exchanged impatient glances.

"Okay. So, what was the dream about, or should I say who. I think we can all guess what kind of dream it was," the major said gravely as if he were discussing the end of the world.

"Oh no, not this again," Alex said. "Look it wasn't that bad, really quite innocent, sort of."

"

"Who was it about?" Samantha asked.

He wanted to tell her it was her and if the major had not been there he might have but he knew that that would be a mistake. If he told them he couldn't remember who it was they would try to hypnotize him and find out who. The perfect answer came to him, Cassandra. They couldn't blame him for thinking about his old girlfriend and if they felt the need to get out there and find her, well that was okay too. He would like to know what had become of her. He suddenly felt terrible having only just really thought about her, after all she had been vegetarian too. It was one of many things that they had had in common. She had been a lot of fun and very beautiful. How bad could it be to see her again?

"Cassandra." He said with conviction. "My girlfriend at the time this all started. She's a vegetarian too. She could be up there somewhere, still alive."

The major looked disappointed, "an old girlfriend. It figures."

Samantha looked disappointed also, she looked away from him and shuffled some papers about.

"We could try to find her," the major said suddenly. "You could take three or four men and try to reach the Bournemouth hotel off Leicester Square. It was turned into a quarantine hospital for people who had come into contact with the virus. She would have been taken there. Once there you could see if they had any files or other information that could be of use to us. We lost contact with them several months ago."

"You didn't send anyone to see what had happened to them?" Alex asked.

"Three different teams, they never came back." The major stood and went to the door. "I'll okay this operation. You will go and look for this girl, no one is to know that she was your girlfriend. We would have chaos if everyone went looking for loved ones now wouldn't we. But as you said, she was vegetarian."

She did eat fish, Alex thought, but he decided not to voice it. It would be good to see her again, at least to have one ally amongst these people who he couldn't quite get along with.

After the major left Samantha sat there for a while not saying anything.

"You all right?" Alex had to ask.

"Of course," she snipped "I was just surprised. I didn't realize that you missed your girlfriend so much or that you were in love with her. You haven't mentioned her once since you've been here."

Alex felt very ashamed.

"There's been so much happening. Time's been difficult for me, it feels as though I've only been here a few days rather than..."

"Many months," Samantha answered.

Another silence descended on them, Alex felt he had driven a wedge between them and wanted to tear it down but he could not.

"Well I did spend much of that time under sedation, if you recall. Where's Caroline?" Alex asked.

"I haven't seen her since yesterday morning, I've been busy. I see more of you than her." She stopped and gathered her things together.

"I'll go and check on her now. See how she is. See you later," she left.

Alex sat there for a while and then decided to check on Caroline for himself. The fact that Samantha would still be there was neither here nor there he told himself.

He reached Caroline's room and knocked, there was no answer. He went in and noticed that the bed did not look as if it had been slept in. The room was bare of all her things. An icy chill traced a spasmodic finger along his spine and he went back into the corridor.

There were no guards in the corridor, he had only just noticed. Some heightened senses I've got, he thought.

He made his way through the dingy passages to the mess hall. He saw few people on the way and he was suddenly aware how the number of people milling around the complex had gone down. The mess hall was empty so he made his way to the control room. That was still guarded by four soldiers which in a strange way gave him a feeling of security. He explained that he wanted access through the key-padded security door. The soldiers buzzed through to get permission to let him in.

The soldier who spoke into the lock system gave him a strange look and then pulled himself up as straight as possible.

"I'm sorry sir. The control room is off limits today."

"Well can you just tell me if Samantha is in there, I need her to help me find someone," Alex said patiently.

The soldier sighed and stooped back down to the entry system phone. He spoke in a whisper which Alex now listened to. The first time he had not paid any attention but this time he was intent on hearing exactly what was going on. He had been through that door on two previous occasions both at the invitation of the major. He knew a lot of things went on in there, perhaps more than he realized. He was still surprised by what he heard.

"Under no circumstances is he to be allowed in. Samantha is here but she is unable to see him. Just tell him that she is not here. Ask him to return to his cell, but call it a room, he can be a bit touchy. Don't bother us again." The entry system gave a metallic edge to the voice that made it seem even more hostile than its words purveyed.

"Sorry sir," the soldier said, his eyes shifted, he was unaccustomed to being ordered to lie. "She's not in there, perhaps you would return to your room and I'll have a call put out for her."

"Um. What about the little girl, Caroline. Is she in there?" Alex folded his arms and looked the man square in the eyes.

The soldier, Alan Smith, his name read, shifted his weight uncomfortably and looked helplessly at the other three. They remained at their posts looking straight ahead but they had seen his wary glance from the corner of their eyes and Alex sensed that their demeanour had now become defensive.

"I'm sorry sir, I can't interrupt them again. Please go back to your room and wait."

"My room? Oh, you mean my cell don't you?"

The soldiers gave up their pretence of non interest and stood either side of Alan, one moved to behind Alex.

"We don't want to hurt you. Please leave the area."

"Are you allowed to hurt me?" Alex asked with genuine curiosity.

Alan was obviously confused.

"You know who I am. Do you?" Alex asked. Now was the time to put his great importance to these people to the test.

"Yes, you are the hybrid," Alan answered before he thought. The hybrid was a name that Alex had become known as behind his back. From his expression, Alan realized that he never heard it before.

"I'm sorry sir. You're Alex Cartier," One of the other soldiers, Mark Whitton had jumped in. He was the youngest of them, probably in his mid twenties.

Alex felt hurt to suddenly find out that he was regarded so contemptuously by people around him. He wondered if Samantha called him the hybrid when he was not around.

A pang of anger hit him in the stomach. "Stand aside," he said as the alarm spread over their faces like warm butter over popcorn.

He was still standing a few feet away from them and they wondered what he had in mind, he wondered too. He could smell the fear.

"I'll try one more time," Alan said and pushed the button in on the speakerphone.

"Er, Alex Cartier needs to come in sir. He is coming in whether we let him or not. What do we do?" There was a silence on the other side of the door.

"Do whatever it takes to get him back to his cell. He is not to enter, full stop."

"But what if we have to shoot him?"

"I told you private, whatever it takes. You can't do him much damage anyway. Make sure you shoot him where it counts or he'll just walk past you" The voice cut off.

Alan raised his rifle and pointed it at Alex, the other three did the same. Alex could almost feel the tip of the gun from a man behind him.

"You gonna shoot me?"

"Not..."

As the man started to speak Alex had wheeled round and disarmed the man behind him. Before the other three could fire, he had knocked them flying in different directions. None of them looked like they would be getting up in a hurry. Alan looked dead, his head was at a strange angle. Alex felt a sickening knot tighten in his stomach. He went over to Alan and found that there was a pulse, though his shoulder was probably dislocated. The others were no threat now.

Alex put his fist through the speakerphone and shorted the wires out then he grasped the handle of the giant door and pulled it open as if it weighed little more than a wooden chair.

He dealt with the three guards as lightly as he could on the other side but still left them in a heap and continued on into the main board room. The man who had been issuing all the orders sat at the table, the rest of the room was empty, it was Seth Richards.

"What the hell do you think you are doing Cartier? You have no right to come in here, messing up my men, I'll have you shot."

"Again?" Alex responded coldly.

Richards looked at him with open contempt, his lean fingers pressed together in front of him. The hate emanated from him invading Alex's aura and sent a double chill down his spine like a rollercoaster, down and up and down again.

"You've stayed out the way, I thought you were dead for some reason."

"You mean you hoped I was dead," Richards said moving his hand to the drawer.

"Can't say I've given you much thought," Alex continued. " Don't bother going for the gun, you know it will be useless." He wasn't sure about that, he just hoped.

Richards sighed and stood up keeping his hands away from his body.

"Why don't we go back to your room and talk about this?"

"Now there's a change of tact." Alex looked past Richards to the door he was guarding.

"What's through there?" Alex asked.

"My washing," Richards said dropping his hands to his side. "How are the men outside, did you kill them?"

"Now, you think of them? Funny it seems out of character for you. I don't kill people who are just doing their job. In fact, I don't kill people." Alex started to move towards the door, Richards stood in front of it and folded his arms.

"You're not going through that door. You would contaminate the people in there and breach our security completely."

"Contaminate? Haven't they done enough tests on me to know I'm safe?"

"Not nearly enough for my liking," Richards said.

Alex chuckled. "You think that you're going to stop me entering that area?"

"I'm appealing to your humanity. You will do unknown harm if you go in. Go back to your room and I'll explain it."

"Explain it now. No, in fact, don't bother to explain it now. Just get out of the way, I don't believe anything you have to say to me. I want to talk to Sam. Bring her out, then, if it's so important that I don't go in."

"Sam? Oh Samantha has left the base."

"Without saying goodbye? Now I know you're lying plus I saw her less than an hour ago. What about Major Hatfield, did he miraculously leave the base also, how?"

"Hatfield has been relieved. I'm in charge."

"Since when?"

"Since always! Now I have decided that the major and Sam's loyalties have been compromised. You may even have infected them."

Alex didn't like the tone he used on Sam's name, it taunted him as if he knew that he cared for her more than he should.

"I've had enough of talking to you." Alex moved forward, Richards reached into his pocket and brought out a hypodermic gun. It fired but Alex avoided it. He grabbed Richards and threw him back in the chair kicking the gun away from him. He wanted to hit him so hard his head would fall off but he was afraid it would, so he backed off.

111

"What was in that?" Alex looked down at the capsule embedded in the wall.

"Enough to kill you hopefully, put you out at the least. Then I could remove your head. I'm sure that would dent your returning from the dead."

"Why didn't you remove my head before?"

"We tried in the later stages but your body had already learnt too much. As fast as we tried to remove it, it healed. Even when you are unconscious your body still protects itself. Now look, I know we've had our problems but you can't do any good here. Go back to your room and I'll come and speak with you later."

Alex swiped him across the face and knocked him out. "Sorry I haven't got any rope on me or I needn't have done that."

He walked to the other door, it was locked. After kicking it open he found himself in a dimly lit tunnel not unlike those of the main complex. On closer inspection he could see strange vents in the ceiling, he had a feeling that nothing was supposed to come out of these tunnels and that the vents were capable of deadly gas if required.

He looked back at Richards. Would he stay out long enough?

Not wishing to take any chances, Alex threw Richards over his shoulder and carried him through the death corridor. If the gas started he wanted Richards there with him.

The door at the end was locked but had a glass panel in it. He could see two guards just inside the door, he put Richards down.

As he crashed through the door and disabled the guards, one of their guns went off, he looked around for anybody else but saw no one.

He stood transfixed at the sight before him. He was in a large hexagonal room with an operating table in the middle. The place was all shiny as if everything was made from stainless steel, apart from the floor which was concrete. There was a large freezer compartment door directly in front of him and several smaller doors on his right. On his left was a large thick glass window. The body of a man was lying by it. He was dressed in white and was presumable one of the scientists working in this lab.

Alex went over to him and rolled him over, he was still alive though he had been shot by the stray bullet from the guard's gun.

Alex's attention was suddenly compelled through the glass window. It looked down into a well lit pit and there lying on a mattress was Caroline. Alex beat on the window but to no avail, she couldn't hear him and was a long way down. There appeared to be only one door into the round pit opposite where Caroline lay, she seemed to be asleep.

Alex grabbed the scientist shaking him as he lifted him up to the glass, the man came round and fear etched itself deep into his face. He started screaming.

"What have you done to her?" Alex shouted his mouth close to the man's face.

"Let me go, get away. You can't help her. It's too late."

"What do you mean?" Alex asked

"Timer mechanism. The door will open in a few minutes, we can't stop it, it's the way the experiments are designed," the man lost consciousness mainly through fear than pain.

Alex tossed him aside, grabbed a jug of water from the operating table, went over to Richards slumped body and tipped it over him.

"Come on Richards. I bet you've got the answers to this."

He dragged Richards over to glass window and pressed his face against it. Blood started to run down window where Richard's nose was squashed to the side.

His eyes blinked a few times, he could hear Alex's voice in his ear and his nose hurt like hell.

Alex dropped him away from the window into a heap on the floor.

"Well, explain it to me."

Richards put a hand up to his nose, the blood was coming out of his mouth as well. He spat on the floor.

"What does it look like you moron?"

"Looks like you've got a child in a big room and something nasty is going to happen in a few minutes." Alex hissed.

"It all works via computer. The timer mechanism is to prevent feelings of guilt from building up in the scientists involved."

"Feelings of guilt?" Alex banged on the glass again trying to wake Caroline up.

"She won't hear you and even you won't break through that," Richards coughed.

"Make it stop." Alex said

"Go back to your room first."

Alex kicked him in the shin.

"I can't stop it. No one can, you just have to let it run its course."

Alex looked around for some kind of control panel. He walked over to the locked doors behind him and wrenched the first one open.

It was an empty cell, one bed, one chair, one toilet. It was empty. He wrenched open the next cell, it was also empty. He glanced back at Richards who refused to meet his gaze.

The last cell gave more resistance but gave in the end.

Samantha was lying on the bunk. She was unconscious, her legs and hands tied. Alex undid the binds and cradled her in his arms. He tapped lightly on her face until her eyes opened and she clasped her arms around him.

He would have pinched himself to make sure he was not dreaming if it hadn't been such a nightmare.

"Caroline!" Samantha said as she tried to push herself up but felt the drugs pushing her back.

Alex carried her out into the hexagonal room up to the glass pit and put her down away from Richards.

"Samantha all right?" Richards asked, surprisingly.

"What do you care?" Alex snapped back.

"She was my fiancée," Richards said with some satisfaction.

Alex felt as though he had been punched in the stomach. Not once had she mentioned a fiancé, but then he realized. Richards was a liar.

"Just give me one reason to kill you. Oh, I forgot," Alex looked through the glass at Caroline, "I already have one."

Samantha managed to get to her feet.

"I'll be all right in a minute, they just hit me with a sedative," she noticed Richards.

"Seth what happened to you?"

"We don't have time to talk about him," Alex said. "How do we get Caroline out of there."

"Major Hatfield! Open the freezer doors!" Sam had just remembered something.

"The freezer doors?" Alex shook his head.

He went over and looked at the keypad to the side.

"The number is four, eight, one, seven," Richards called. "No reason for you to destroy another perfectly good door."

"It's four, eight, two, four. I saw them putting him in," Samantha said. She glowered at Richards. "Alex is on our side."

"Which side are you on?" Richards asked, with a look of hurt in his eyes.

Alex punched in the figures and the door opened. There were two sides to the locker, one had human bodies, the other creature types. Hatfield was just sitting on the floor.

"They pushed him in there, they refused to take his orders, he wanted the experiments shutdown. I didn't know what was going on here, they would have put me in there to but..." she looked at Richards. "You stopped them. You've been controlling all this."

"Somebody has to be in control that can make harsh decisions. The human race may be at stake here, not just some tiny place called Britain," Richards said.

Alex had moved Hatfield out of the locker.

"He's still alive."

Samantha grabbed some medical items from a cupboard under the operating table and injected him with something.

"He should make it." She started to cry. "Caroline, we can't help her."

"Where is the main computer?' Alex asked.

"Way back in the complex," Richards responded. His nose had stopped bleeding and it didn't seem broken as he had feared. "You'd never reach it in time."

Alex grabbed a weapon from one of guards.

"I wouldn't do that if I were you," Richards said.

Alex fired at the glass. The bullets bounced off and ricocheted around the room narrowly missing Samantha and the major. The scientist on the floor was not so lucky and caught one in the leg.

"Is that how you intend to kill all of us?" Richards asked "By wounding us to death."

A red light began to pulsate in the ceiling and a computer voice announced that there was one minute to go.

Alex glanced back at the freezer.

"Where did you get those creatures from?"

"They fell down the shaft when you blew the doors off on that little escapade a few weeks ago. We've had a few topple down, they just don't seem to learn. They always survive the fall but they're not impossible to kill, like you are."

"They survive the fall? How? They don't fall down, they climb down, they want you to take them in." Alex realized they were looking for him.

"Door release in five seconds," the metallic voice said.

"Five, four, three, two, one."

Alex and Samantha looked through the window. Caroline had woken up and was standing next to the mattress looking around. She looked up and saw them, relief flooded her face, and then the door clicked open on the other side of the room.

One of the creatures ambled into the room. It was more humanoid looking than before. It was like a zombie but still with the taloned hands and the sharp pointed teeth. His eyes were a clear green, it was not blind. Its nose twitched as it moved into the room towards Caroline. Its front limbs were still arms but the hind legs bent the wrong way though it stood erect. She remained very still hardly daring to breathe.

Alex grabbed a handgun and put it to Richard's temple.

"She dies, you die. How do I stop it?"

Richards looked at him contemptuously and yet there was a glimmer of doubt that played around his eyes.

"It won't hurt her. It's not the first one that's been in there."

Alex cocked the gun and let his finger pull the trigger.

"No!" Samantha knocked his hand away, the bullet ricochetted off the glass again and finally embedded itself in the unlucky scientist.

"He must be like a magnet for those things," Richard said as Alex knocked him to the floor.

They watched helplessly as the creature advanced on Caroline. It looked up and saw Alex looking down at it. Amazement clouded its face then it let out a scream and advanced on the girl. This one was hungry.

Alex ran back from the glass and then ran towards it leaping and kicking at the same time while he thought, I must get through this.

Samantha moved back as he hit the glass but she noticed that the glass cracked even before he touched it.

The glass showered down on the creature and Caroline who had taken refuge under her mattress. Alex landed between them, the creature stopped its advance and howled in pain at a large chunk of glass embedded in its thigh. The remnants of the clothes it was wearing were army issue and the dog tag it still wore said Alan Smith. Alex had little time to think how this had happened, it launched itself at him, and its hands sought his throat. He held it at bay and his hands felt for its throat, then he wrung the neck so hard that the head twisted off and lay in a bloody heap at this side. Caroline crawled from under the mattress and ran to his side. He was vaguely aware of an alarm sound going off in the death corridor and the computer calling for immediate shutdown of the area. Then the lights went out and the hiss of gas could be heard coming from the ceiling.

Chapter 10

Daniel found that he could swim very fast. There was a new strength in his arms and legs which he had not felt before. The ship was waiting for him, they were waiting, Katrina waited. As fast as he swam, the torpedo overtook him, he felt it sail by and cursed Ben for the lack of trust. He was only fifty metres from the ship when it blew up, pieces of wood rained down on him, a severed hand slapped him on the face and nearly knocked him out. He gulped down some sea water and felt himself go under, he was dropping like a dead weight, through the darkness, the cold skin of the water enveloped him, his arms reached up for the last fragments of sunlight and he made a mental note to swim up to it but something was pulling him down. His arms were not his own, nor his legs, it was as if his body belonged to another and it was determined that he sink to the bottom.

Sea water filled his mouth, panic penetrated his fear and he managed to thrash wildly around and then he realized, he was not drowning. Although it was uncomfortable, he was able to take in the water and expel it through his ears. Something within his sinuses was allowing him to glean oxygen from it like a fish.

He hit something below him which felt like hard metal and found himself sprawled out on a flat object below him. He lay there for some time looking up towards the sunlight which was probably less than a hundred metres away. He felt a thump next to him on the metal, Slayman had landed next to him. The look of surprise on Slayman's face was almost comical as he raised a taloned finger to the black hole in his head where his eye had once looked malevolently on the world, his other eye firmly fixed on Daniel's face. A smile played across his lips in the blue light and his tongue darted in and out. Slayman had grown somehow. He still had a human shape but it had plumped up, his whole physique was bigger, taller more muscular or a trick of the water.

Slowly, Daniel moved away from Slayman, he wondered what his chances were of making it back to the top when the metal plate below him moved. A door had opened up in the sunken spaceship and all the bodies, alive and dead were taken aboard.

The sea water gushed into a receiving chamber and then the hatch closed and the water pumped away. Daniel stood up, glad to find himself on solid ground again, Slayman stood also. Two others were dead, one with his head missing, the other only had one leg but they seem to be protecting something they were covering with misshapen bodies. It was Katrina.

He forgot Slayman for a moment, rushed to her side and pulled her from the macabre protection she had been given.

"Is she alive?" Slayman's voice was cold, uncaring, he requested only information.

"Yes, she is alive. Why are you still alive?" Daniel answered as he picked Katrina up and carried her as far from Slayman as the circular room would allow.

"It takes a lot to kill us," Slayman responded, "but not, apparently as much as it would take to kill you. You have us all wrong."

"Us? Who are us? Murdering thieves who profit from killing endangered species? Or vicious psychopathic aliens"

Slayman laughed and shook his head at the same time. "The man you knew is practically gone, the part of me that was him is little more than a cell now, his brain and all other bodily functions are completely mine. He is no more than a virus which in time will completely leave my body."

"What are you?" Daniel asked.

"Well, we are inside a SPACESHIP!" Slayman flapped his arms wildly around. "You are supposed to know all about us. You are supposed to be our key to survival here. You are supposed to be the Menarty," Slayman gave an impatient snort, "it is obvious to me that you are not." He sank down onto the floor and scratched his head. The talons bit into his scalp and caused it to bleed.

Daniel cradled Katrina's body in his arms, she looked small and pale, her breathing was slow. "Is she still human?" Daniel asked.

"She is supposedly the Narquet," Slayman replied dismissively.

"Menarty, Narquet, are you going to explain that to me?" Daniel saw Slayman flinch from the annoyance in his voice.

"Well why not," he replied with a grimace of a smile. "It is written in our prophecies that four people will be our main allies on this planet. It is through them that we will rule and eventually extinguish any full-blooded human that does not capitulate to us: Menarty, he who will enforce our reign by guiding us to victory through his psychic means; Narquet, she who will secure our future by bearing a child more than endorsed with the strengths of both cultures, fathered by Menarty; Misanthorpe, the wise one who has all knowledge and the secrets to defeat our enemies; and Rugron, the destroyer of dreams who will kill our enemies and lead us to everlasting victory."

"And you think that I am one of these?" Daniel wiped some dry salt from his mouth.

"No, I do not," Slayman hissed, "but others think you are and we are a democratic race."

Daniel snorted. "Mind reading does not allow for much democracy."

"You are supposed to be Menarty, he who will lead us and enforce our reign," Slayman stifled a chuckle and glanced dismissively at Katrina. "She is supposed to be Narquet, the bearer of new blood who will carry Menarty's child."

Daniel said nothing. He looked up at the closed hatch above them and wondered if there was some way of opening it. Some way to escape before they found out that they had the wrong people.

"It is written in our books, that Menarty would love Narquet so much that he would rather kill a thousand of his own kind than see one hair on her head harmed. That she would be of the purest soul, uncorrupted and peaceful, that a light would shine around her and make all those she met weep with joy."

He pointed his taloned finger again and said, "She is not Narquet and you are not in love with her. You protect her merely because she is the female of the species and you care for her. However, there is a big difference between caring for someone and loving them more than life itself."

"What would you know about love, decency or any of our planet's inhabitants? You are just a few drooling monsters from space that lost your way and decided to try to take over the nearest planet. You know nothing of honour or friendship, love or hate. But I have a feeling that you will learn about hate pretty quickly. Besides, if you're so sure that I am not Menarty, what does it matter whether I love Katrina or not? She could still be Narquet, you may have just got the wrong man."

"I am not sure about you yet, you may just be misguided," Slayman said, "but I'm ninety-nine per cent sure that she is not Narquet," Slayman grinned exposing his jagged imp-like teeth. "When I am sure about you, you will know."

"So let's talk about this spaceship," Daniel said as he walked around tapping on the walls.

"You want to know how long it has been here. How we landed without detection? Let me tell you something about my people, we are not to be underestimated."

"Why do you need humans to lead you?" Daniel tapped at the metal; it gave a deep booming response.

"It is part of our culture. It is written that when we relocate to a new planet, we will find our leaders there. And by ingesting the brains of our enemies, we will know their knowledge. That we must return to an earlier time in our evolvation and evolve again along a different path that matches our chosen planet."

"I don't think the word evolvation exists," Daniel murmured as he returned to Katrina's side. He had finished tapping the walls and had discovered a sectional flap, which concealed a panel beneath it. Slayman did not seem remotely interested with what he was doing.

"I am sorry, I use the language of the host, perhaps his English wasn't so good."

"No, he was German." Daniel sat down next to Katrina torn by the desire to kill Slayman or to learn more about them.

"So you're a parasitic civilisation, advanced enough for space travel that communicate through ESP, a cross between the Go'uld and the Borg."

Slayman became alarmed, "there are others here that fight for this planet?"

"Didn't your host watch television?" Daniel said with some contempt sifting through into his voice.

Slayman recoiled as if hit by something, his eyes blackened and then returned to green.

"Is the host still there?" Daniel wondered how he would tell. There had been little difference between the captain and a parasitic monster from hell.

"When we merge, we become one with the host. Their body becomes our body, their mind our mind, we are still that person in a way, but much more than they could ever imagine. Perhaps my host didn't watch television"

"How do you spread?" Daniel had wanted to say contaminate but he changed his mind.

We are liquid in base, minute complex organisms. A glass of water could contain as many as a thousand of us. We are here because our planet died and we need yours."

"Seawater or fresh water?"

"Seawater. Fresh water was unknown to us before we came to this planet but we see from the people we have taken over to our side that there is much fresh water here. That must be turned to salt water that we may thrive forever."

"How did little pellets of water fly a spaceship or even invent a spaceship?

"By using the last remaining hosts from Visirus Seven. They were most useful vessels but unfortunately they had a very short lifespan which even our healing properties could not elongate."

"Elongate? Let's hope you're not chosen to be their spokes creature."

"Just think how much of this planet is sea water, we deserve to live here. This is our chosen place that we have searched for, for thousands of years. Already our armies are waiting in the sea to become one with their new bodies."

"I swallowed some sea water back there, does that mean that I will turn into a drooling pointed teeth ghoul?"

"You know you won't. You are immune because of a number of factors, many that we can't determine and that make you a good candidate for Menarty. Others are immune because they have no meat in their stomachs. When we enter a human we must find the stomach and use the meat within to take over the person. Once we start we can take over the body in stages. We become more refined in the way we do this as we evolve."

"What about eating the brains of those you don't want?"

"It's all a question of intelligence. We gain knowledge from the vessel we take the food from. Not because we are consuming their brain, that is just a physical act to help with the psychic one which takes place at the same time, sucking the experiences and the knowledge from the creature until they are dead. In this way we can learn about everything very quickly. You can have no secrets from us, we will always find out by digesting someone who knows." Slayman shook his head. "There have been some teething problems," he smiled at his own pun.

"In what way?" Daniel asked.

"Well, a couple of our kind were told they could eat each other's brains, this made them feel ill and obviously there was no gain to the knowledge we held so that was a mistake. They were overcome by the power of another who has not yet embraced his future, as you also have not. It is written that we will nearly kill our chosen ones many times before they take their true place in our culture, before their minds allow us in and they lead us to domination."

"So you don't really know who you are looking for. Every time you see someone chewing on a piece of lettuce, you have to think, is this our leader?"

"You're not listening to me. It is not enough just to have no meat in their stomach, they have something more, as you do."

"So if I were to suddenly eat a piece of meat, you could possess me?
"

"No, the subject must have meat ingrained in their system. If you were a meat eater and just stopped eating it today, it could take more than five years for all the meat to leave your system, therefore, any vegetarian we find who has not been so for a few years is prone to become part of our society. Just in case you thought that by everyone switching from meat, they would immediately be immune."

"So you have to be careful that you don't kill your chosen ones, that is going to make is hard to kill people on mass."

"Yes, we must find our chosen ones for once we do, this planet will be ours."

"Supposing you don't find them, or kill them by accident or they don't want to join you, what then?"

"Then a war will rage on Earth until the other prophecies have been fulfilled."

"I'd be interested in reading about your culture with a view to learning more about you," Daniel winced, it hadn't sounded convincing. "Especially a culture that has back up prophecies, in case their first ones don't work out."

"You would like to see our holy books? I wonder why," Slayman said sarcastically and smiled and they both knew that Daniel thought only of their destruction. "You see, the four we seek will be against us in the beginning until they see how advanced we really are and that to be a part of us is their destiny. Once they understand that we are a good people, they will want to lead us."

"Still, it is going to make it tough for you. Everyone hating you, everyone trying to kill you, and you trying to convince them that you come in peace with someone's brain dripping from the side of your mouth, so sad."

"I never said that we came in peace," Slayman's eyes turned black for a moment and then he continued, "there are many on your planet who will be pleased just to join us, to work for us, to do our labor."

"Didn't I skewer your eye? Did it regenerate or did you just steal someone else?"

"If you look closely you will see that my eyes are now slightly different colours. It would have regenerated but I did not have the time to wait so I procured another one from elsewhere."

Katrina started to wake up and screamed as her eyes fell on Slayman, Daniel leapt to her side and held her tightly until her screams turned to sobs and then she was quiet. She gazed up at him with sorrowful eyes her nose running and a little scratch on her cheek.

"It's okay, we're…" Daniel thought about saying spaceship and changed his mind, neither did it seem wise to point out that they were still in the sea, who knows how far down, "safe," he finished and glanced at Slayman who smiled openly at him.

"Where are we?" She asked

"Safe," Slayman said barely able to contain himself as an odd guttural chuckle issued forth.

"I don't feel too good, I feel as though I have something in my stomach pounding against the wall trying to get out," Katrina said softly in short gasps.

Daniel looked over to Slayman and realized that he seemed surprised at this. His eyes went black and he once again communicated with the rest of his kind.

"I feel so sick," Katrina said and immediately threw up a brownish liquid mixed with large splashed of brilliant red.

"What the hell's wrong with her?" Daniel demanded as he lay her down and lifted her t- shirt to inspect her stomach. It was moving from the inside.

"If something pops out of her stomach you'll be dead as well," Daniel hissed.

Slayman walked over and went to lay his taloned fingers on the pulsating stomach. Daniel almost pushed him away but saw from his eyes that he wanted to help, he was confused about this sudden malady.

Slayman's eyes went black again as he focussed on what we happening inside. He broke off and backed away.

"Well, what is it?" Daniel shouted at him with the threat of death in his eyes.

"She must have swallowed a shoal of our beings. It is most unfortunate and an unlikely occurrence as there aren't that many shoals out here."

"What are you talking about?" Daniel said exasperated, Katrina was coughing up more blood.

"As I said before, we are minute beings living in the sea at present waiting for hosts. We stay together in a shoal until a host is accessible and then one breaks off and claims the host. It appears that Katrina has swallowed a whole group, maybe fifty or more and they are confused, they don't understand what has happened and are fighting for the body."

"The body?"

"If she is the Narquet, she will survive, of this we are sure. On the other hand."

Katrina sat bolt upright as blood and water issued forth from her mouth. The water particles extricated themselves from the blood drifted apart on the floor of the spaceship seemingly with a life of their own and then drifted back together and remained motionless in a small puddle of seawater.

"They are trying to get out of her body as there is no meat to sustain them within it. Once they have entered they must find sustenance immediately or leave before they starve," Slayman said as he moved to the wall panel and pushed a button which allowed the ceiling to open. A force field kept the sea water from flooding in.

Katrina's eyes turned black and her throat constricted, blood began to leak from her ears as seawater gushed from her nose as though a tap had been turned on with the force of Niagara Falls.

"Help her!" Daniel cried, he wheeled round to Slayman who was about to push another button.

"We have to let them get back in the sea," he said calmly, "or they will mutate."

"If you release that force field we will have tons of water on us," Daniel said with some menace in his voice.

"So we will, but I will survive so would the Narquet and the Menarty and who knows you may too." He pushed the button and the shield dropped away, the water crashed in, the whole ship moved with the force.

It felt like a steel girder had dropped on Daniel as he struggled to hold onto Katrina. Thirty entities left her body at the same time from whichever pore they were nearest taking skin and flesh with them, it was as if she were torn apart from the inside in their desperation to return to the sea. The ship abruptly stopped and threw him upwards into the dark void, away from Katrina's remains and Slaymans crushed and broken body. Daniel called her name in the darkness as he was propelled towards the surface, the pressure on his body and within him threatening to tear him apart. His head felt like it must explode and then he was floating looking up at the sky, unable to move his limbs, taking gulps of seawater every now and then as the waves rode over him. For hours he floated, unable to move until he felt his bones click back into place, his mind was still grieving for Katrina whom he had promised to protect and yet been unable to. As feeling returned to his arms, he found he was able to swim. Though he had no idea where he might swim to until he spotted a small fishing boat and headed towards it.

They spotted him in the water and took him aboard but he could not speak to them or tell them what he had been through, he could only stare blankly ahead and wonder what lay ahead and how the rest of the world was fairing.

Eventually he managed to convey that he was an American and it was not long after that that he found himself on an aeroplane bound for the states. He had hardly spoken a word to anyone except to ask to be taken home. He knew that there was a new sort of war brewing, one that had never been fought before, that people would turn on their own kind and that the probable outcome would be the destruction of the Earth or the life forms on it.

He carried within him more than one secret and more than one answer, his mind was in calm, he focussed all his energy on his captive. The small entity that swam round in his stomach and looked for escape where there was none. He held it in place with the will of his mind determined to get something back for study which would be worth the life of Katrina and the others.

He could not eat or drink until he had discharged his prisoner and he could not do that until he had the right conditions.

Even as he looked out of the window of the aeroplane, high above the clouds in the blueness of the sky he heard it talking to him. It called him Menarty and asked to be released, to be spat out into the ocean or to be allowed to leave his body via his sweat but Daniel ignored its pleas for help and revelled in its claim that it suffered greatly and was starving.

"Can I get you something?" The stewardess asked, her concern showed around her eyes.

"Just some salt and a quarter glass of water," Daniel replied.

The woman nodded and returned with a few packets of salt and the water.

Daniel added them together and drank the salt water quickly. The taste made him want to throw up but he resisted with every ounce of will power he possessed, it wanted to get out of him, it didn't care how. He just wanted to keep it alive long enough for the scientists to get a good look.

"Thank you Menarty for the salt," he heard it say in his head and he smiled.

Chapter 11

"We've got to get out and now," Richards called down. "That's our only way out!" he indicated where the creature had come from.

"Samantha I'll lower you down," Richards offered his hand.

"What about Hatfield?
"

"He's too heavy, we don't have the time," the hissing sound of gas was getting louder heavy cloud was making its way from the ceiling. "The corridor will be worse. There's no way back to my office, only through there. We can get out at the holding centre. That was the only creature we had left. The holding centre will be empty now. Move!"

"Not without Hatfield," Samantha struggled with Hatfield trying to get him to stand then Alex was with them.

"How the hell did you get back from down there?" Asked Richards.

"I jumped," Alex said as he slung Hatfield's body over his shoulder and leapt back down again. Next he returned for Samantha, he picked her up as if he were carrying her over the threshold and jumped back into the pit. Hatfield and Caroline had started to move slowly through the open door on the other side of the pit.

"It's dark!" Caroline called back.

"It's all right, I can see," Alex said as he put Samantha down.

"Hey, I need some help here, I can't jump thirty feet," Richards called.

"Let's go," Alex said to the others.

Samantha stopped and looked back, "You can't leave him, he'll be killed."

"I should go back for the scientist guy. I didn't mean for him to get hit with a bullet." Alex went back and leapt up. Richards was stooped near the ground coughing, the gas was nowhere near yet. The scientist was dead, he looked at Richards and grudgingly took him down into the pit.

When all of them were in the tunnel, they closed the door to the arena and Alex led the way slowly along the black passage.

"How come the gas doesn't go off in this tunnel Richards?" Alex asked.

"Good question," Richards replied. "we hadn't finished installing it."

"Just as well."

A light started to appear at the end of the tunnel, Alex helped Hatfield along with Richards at the back. Alex stopped and looked back.

"I think you should go first, just in case," he waited for Richards to make his way to the front. The tunnel was narrow and it was difficult for him to get past Hatfield but with some effort and shoving he managed it.

"Happy now, I am in the lead." Richards moved slowly forward towards the light which emanated from under a large wooden door.

Richards opened the door into a brightly lit area. Straw beds were on the floor and raw meat lay scattered around.

"Nobody home," he said as he moved into the middle of the holding centre.

The others moved up beside him and closed the door when they were all through.

"Well superman, what now?" Richards said

They were in another arena, the glass panel was thirty feet up and they could not see any movement on that side.

"Can't you let them know we're here," Samantha asked.

"How, that glass is sound proof and as they don't have any subjects. Although the lights are on, they must be about to do something. Perhaps they caught another one." Richards became agitated.

"We've got to get out of here before they put it in with us."

Alex looked around, "How do the they get them in here, the only door is the way we came?"

As if in response a panel opened on the glass above them, it must have been two foot thick and a creature was pushed through. It fell heavily on the ground narrowly missing Richards who dived out of the way and then scurried to the furthest point away from the writhing thing.

Its leg had broken on the way down and the humanlike qualities were in a grimace of pain. It took a while to comprehend that it was not alone in the arena.

Samantha was waving at the faces she could now see above them looking through the glass. She indicated Major Hatfield and couldn't stop herself from shouting when the faces moved away.

"They won't let us out," Richards said "it would be a breach of security especially now we have this thing in here. He slumped against the wall and slid down to sit on the rough sand below him.

Several more faces had now appeared at the window, they looked very concerned and from their lip movement it appeared that there was a lot of shouting going on.

"Can you hear what they are saying?" Richards asked.

"No," Alex lied, he could hear some muffled sounds and the occasional word. It didn't sound good.

"How does this setup work?" Alex asked.

"The creatures get down the elevator shaft, but before they can reach the base they find themselves detoured along a trap corridor, as soon as one goes down it, doors close cutting off its retreat. It soon finds itself in this glass tunnel which brings it out here."

"It looked like it was thrown down here," Samantha said.

"It works on wind, high velocity moves along the tunnel and pushes them over the edge. They frequently get damaged on the way down but they soon heal," Richards voice softened. It was the first time Alex had heard him speak with some compassion.

"Are you all right Sam, you know I wouldn't allow anything to happen to you," Richards said.

"Well this appears to be something," Alex said as he helped Major Hatfield to the opposite side of the area as the creature which still watched them with an almost quizzical expression.

The faces at the window above had doubled, they were frightened, they could see some of their top people trapped in a test area and they did not know what to do. A voice infiltrated the silence.

"Mr Richards, we are unable to let you out this way but perhaps you could go back the way you came," they couldn't see who was talking but he sounded young.

Richards looked up at the ceiling, he could see a speaker and he guessed they would be listening now. "What about the gas?"

"It's gone, we've stopped it and secured the area. Dr Frost was dead"

"Yes, he got shot by accident," Richards glanced at Alex.

"Are you infected sir?" the young voice asked.

"No of course not," Richards replied as sarcastically as he could. "Would I tell you if I was?"

"Well, what do we do?"

"Just wait," Richards answered.

"Sir there's another two creatures on their way through the tunnel. We can't stop the system, it's automated you know, they'll end up in there with you. I'm sorry."

"More coming?" Caroline squeaked.

"Some system," Alex murmured. "At least get Samantha out."

"We can't. Don't you think I would if I could, she's my fiancée."

"Was yours," Alex said his neck prickling.

"Hey, let's think about getting Caroline out," Samantha said.

"We can't. She was the original test subject. We were trying to find out why they didn't hurt her," Richards said.

"Because they weren't bloody hungry," Alex said as he advanced on Richards.

"Stop, this won't do any good." Samantha was about to say more when the glass door opened above them and two more creatures were propelled into the arena.

One of them was not hurt, it picked itself up and looked around. These were definitely different to the ones Alex had seen guarding the bus. Although their eyes were dark and the fingers were talons, there was a more humanoid character in their face. Their teeth remained uneven and jagged but their hair remained. The hind legs still bent the wrong way but they had human arms. The one that was unhurt stood facing them across the expanse of sand. The scientists watched from above.

"Are these hungry?" Richards asked.

Major Hatfield stood up and spoke, "Find a way to get us out of here or you'll all be court-martialled. Is that clear?"

"You're not in command any more sir. I'm sorry," the voice came back. "Only Mr Richards can make the decisions."

Hatfield looked at Richards. "You're in my country on my base, you will tell them to do as I instruct you."

Richards shook his head. "Don't you think I want to get out of here? I can't risk contaminating the rest of the base. I'm prepared to die for that, you should be too."

"When we get out of this, I'll have you court-martialled, imprisoned and possibly executed." Hatfield sank back to the ground again.

"I'm not in the military Major. That was just a cover. I couldn't allow you stop the experiments and I am sorry for using Caroline. We didn't think she was in any real danger. After all they had kept her alive on the surface."

"As a decoy, you idiot," Alex said.

The creature moved forward and everyone moved against the wall behind Alex. The second creature moved forward, it appeared to have a broken arm.

141

"Three more creatures on their way!" The voice over the intercom sounded alarmed. "Should I release the gas sir?" The voice was broken.

"Gas," Alex growled and glanced at Richards while he kept most of his attention on the two creatures in front of him.

"There are gas vents in the ceiling. It would kill everything in here, except Cartier perhaps."

"You can't tell them to do that," Samantha said her eyes gleaming.

Richards looked at her and then reached over and took her hand.

"Hold on the gas," he said loudly. "Wait to see if we are infected."

"Or eaten alive," Caroline murmured.

The creatures had moved to the middle of the arena, they glanced at one another and kept turning their full attention to Alex. He was sure they were trying to communicate with him but he couldn't hear them.

"Hungry," the one on the floor said.

"Now they talk?" Samantha whispered.

"Hungry," the other two responded in unison.

They picked up nearby meat, sniffed it and then tossed it aside, they seemed at a loss as to what to do next.

142

"Aren't these your buddies?" Richards asked.

"One tried to kill me a little while ago or weren't you watching," Alex hissed.

"No, I missed that, could you get these to try it again, I'll make sure I see it all this time."

The first creature pointed at Caroline.

"Food?" It said in a low guttural voice.

"No." Replied Alex.

The first creature looked at the second, they seemed to have a silent conversation then it pointed at Major Hatfield. "Food!" It sounded more insistent.

"No," Alex replied helplessly.

The creature put a talon up to its head and seem to scratch it as though it were trying to get its brain to work. It pointed at Richards. "Food," it sounded desperate this time there was no question mark at the end.

Alex hesitated.

"Alex," Samantha hissed.

"I'm thinking," Alex replied.

"You gonna watch while they crush my skull and eat my brains," Richards said bitterly. "How long do you think it will be before they gas the place if that happens?"

The creature had started to move forward just as three more were propelled through the glass door. They all stood up unharmed. They looked as advanced as the one that was now advancing on Richards.

"No, not food," Alex said stepping forward.

The creature hesitated and then moved back to the others. The five that were unhurt huddled together as though they were discussing something of great importance.

"What are they talking about," Richards asked Alex.

"Football, picking up girls, you know the usual."

"Alex you're not helping," Samantha said.

"How should I know what they are talking about," Alex realized that Richards still held Samantha's hand, she in turn had Caroline's and Hatfield was on the other side.

"Hey Timmy," Alex had decided to name the leader.

"Timmy?'Hatfield said.

"It's better than calling it 'Creature One,' isn't it?" Alex moved forward.

"Can you say anything other than hungry?
"

"Hungry," Timmy replied.

"Okay, what about your friend there with the broken leg, Couldn't you eat him?"

"Alex what are you saying?" Samantha asked.

"He's wounded anyway and they have to eat." Alex said.

Timmy looked at the wounded creature and then back at Alex. "Food?" it asked, indicating the damaged creature.

Alex hesitated, he hadn't expected them to take notice of what he said in quite such a literal way. Now that he was being asked to condemn the wounded creature, he found he couldn't.

"No, I was just saying he needed food too."

The creature looked at him, its eyes seemed to bore right into him and then it indicated the wounded creature to the others. They grabbed it, pinned it down and ripped away with their talons until it was just a bloody mess.

"What have you done," Richards cried. "Turned them into cannibals."

"I didn't mean."

"Perhaps it's for the best" Hatfield said. "If they start eating their own, there will be less of them fight. I'd say it was a good call."

The sound of the creatures eating was awful. Richards pulled Samantha to him, she buried her head in his shoulder to try to keep out the sound. Caroline was held by Major Hatfield, she looked blankly ahead trying to imagine herself somewhere else. Alex felt completely alone.

Why hadn't he let them eat Richards he thought and looked up at the flurry of excitement above him.

"You enjoying this," he shouted up, "plenty to write soon in your little note books."

"Five more coming in!" The voice screamed.

"You sure you're not letting them in?" Alex shouted back.

The other creatures understood and moved away from the area where the new ones would fall.

"It's getting crowded in here. You've got to get us out," Major Hatfield said. "lets go back the way we came, take a gamble that the gas has gone. It's better than staying here."

Two more creatures dropped down into the arena. They glanced at the ripped creature and at the others. Tim seemed to be explaining things to them with his eyes. They nodded as though they already knew and all of them faced Alex across the arena.

"Where's the other three?" Samantha asked.

"Perhaps they got lost," Alex said.

"Perhaps they got out," Hatfield said.

"Ten more on their way," the voice came over the intercom.

Richards stepped forward and opened his mouth, Alex knew he was about to give the order to release the gas in the holding pit. He moved back and caught Richards with his elbow knocking him out.

Samantha knelt down by Richards side. "Why did you do that Alex? Whose side are you on?"

"He was about to kill all of us," Alex replied.

"Not you, you're immune, it would take an atom bomb to get you and then we'd have to decapitate the body," Samantha said as she cradled Richards head in her lap.

Alex was shocked and hurt by her words, Caroline started to cry.

"I'm sorry Caroline," Samantha was saying, "I didn't mean it."

"Are there really ten more creatures on their way here?" Caroline asked barely able to speak the words.

"No, they've gone out to eat." Alex replied. He knew they had already found another way out into the base. Somehow every creature that had come down here had passed on information to others, now they had escaped the tube somewhere. He thought about smashing through and getting to the lift shaft, then they could get to the surface.

"Twenty more have entered the ……..Ahh." The voice trailed off. The creatures were in the control room. The next faces they saw at the glass looking down on them were barely human.

Tim moved forward, it pointed at Samantha, Caroline, Hatfield and Richards, "Not food" it said.

The others nodded.

It looked down at the corpse of their former comrade, "bad food," it said.

Alex realized that it could have said these things to the others without speaking but it wanted him to know, it wanted him to understand. They regarded him with hostile but questioning eyes. He had told them to eat bad meat, perhaps he was not what they thought.

Richards had come round on the floor. "Gas. Turn on the gas," he shouted.

"They can't hear you," Alex said. "You're not in control anymore. They are," he indicated Tim, who smiled in return.

Chapter 12

Daniel was taken to Washington on his arrival in the USA. Security was tight around him and he had to undergo a number of unpleasant tests before he was taken seriously and moved to the Pentagon where some knowledge of the invaders was already known. He had not yet told them of the one in liquid form which he carried in his stomach, he wanted to be sure first that he was talking to the top of the command chain and that they realized how valuable he was to them. He did not relish having his stomach cut open to extract the alien and felt sure that as he could communicate with it, he could persuade it to leave via a tear duct or some spittle into a nice glass of seawater.

He had managed to get a regular supply of salt water without drawing the scientists attention to the fact that he was not eating his food but just drinking the water with the table salt. He did not feel that they were ready yet for all the knowledge he possessed, besides, he was getting use to the creature within him, he learnt much from what it told him, though he was not sure whether to believe it or not.

His clearance had to be upgraded so that he could speak with the people that needed his help and he was surprised to learn that by the time he had reached Washington, England and some of Europe were believed to be completely contaminated.

It had first come to light six months ago in England, one of the top CIA men, Seth Richards, had been in charge of the complex below Centre Point in Tottenham Court Rd, they had not heard from him for some time. But they knew he had found a man who was like Daniel, but affected in a very different way, it made him stronger and difficult to kill with such healing powers that his body regenerated almost as it was wounded. Daniel knew his name even before they told it to him, it was Alex Cartier. The creature within him had told him that this Cartier person could be another of the prophetic personalities they sought. It had no other information on him, except that he had last been seen leaving the complex with a child and a woman. The creature also said that the child was not human but that Cartier and the woman believed she was.

Daniel had pressed the creature on more information about the child, was she one of them? No, it had thought back to him, "she is one of the others."

Daniel was introduced to Mr Sloane, chief in charge of extra terrestrial communications and defence. A tall man with far too many worry lines than his fifty years should have given him. He had listened patiently to all that Daniel said and had been particular scared by the seawater method of infection. Daniel had wondered at the way Sloane had stared at him. Did he know that he carried a creature within him, was there the inkling of an idea forming in his brain or had he just had a heavy dinner?

They had their sessions in the oval office, Daniel enjoyed it and the president was never around. Probably no coincidence.

"Tell me again how you managed to get away from the space ship under the sea," Sloane asked for the hundredth time.

"You make it sound like a fairy story," Daniel replied, his patience almost gone.

"It's just that we have only your testimony that we are dealing with aliens. In fact it seems more like we are dealing with a devastating virus possibly created by man and spread in the free world."

"The free world? America? It's not even here yet! If that's your theory, that it's manmade, then it must have originated from here, since we seem to be the last country in the world to be infected by it."

"Not the last, Canada, Mexico, several island countries, though we have lost contact with a great deal of the world, however, Australia has yet to show any signs, there are also few cases reported in Asia or Africa. But then we are not getting any reports from those areas."

"Well, there's still hope," Daniel said, his head starting to throb.

"Look, I'm on your side, you are our most important member of the team," Sloane paused to make sure that he had gained Daniel's attention.

"The team?"

"A new division we have set up. It consists of one hundred highly trained soldiers, all vegetarian, myself, a couple of other secret members in the government and yourself. "We are being called Dead landers."

"Dead landers?"

"Yes, it is our job to go out and and see what contamination has occurred in the world and if a country or area has been infected beyond repair, we will declare it a Dead land and make sure that there is no life on it of any kind." Sloane waited while the information sank in. "We would also have liked Alex Cartier to have been part of the team as the intelligence we received on him before our loss of communications with Britain was astounding. However, Britain looks like the first major casualty and we have no way of reaching him or even finding out if he is still alive."

"I might be able to help you with that, if you give me more time," Daniel sent an urgent message to the guest in his stomach but received no reply.

"We don't have more time, we leave for New York tomorrow. You'd better eat something before we go."

Daniel shrugged, "Supposing I don't want to be part of your team, a destroyer of countries, murderer of survivors."

"First we need to find out if that is you speaking or whatever is within you."

Daniel went pale, he was about to deny the creature within when four men in white coats entered the room. How could they know about it, he thought.

"I have psychic powers," Sloane said without any flourish or emphasis, he might as well have been talking about shopping. "I hear it talking to you and you answering back. And let me say it is because I have heard you these last few days that I know you are loyal to Earth. However I think it may be contaminating your judgement and may even be trying to kill you by letting you starve to death rather than leave your body which I sense it could do anytime."

Daniel tried to get up but the men dressed in white held him in the chair.

"Just how do you think you are going to get it out of me," Daniel said as a pain seared through his stomach. The creature was trying to get into his blood stream.

"Swallow the pill," Sloane said as a tube was rammed down his throat and a tablet flew down his throat. The men put a metallic bowl in front of him, it contained salt water.

"What…?"

The next moment it felt as though his stomach was turning inside out, everything within it was flying up through his throat and into the bowl.

"You idiot," he managed to say after coughing his stomach lining up, "I could communicate with it, I was able to know what they were doing. I could have found Mason."

Blood was now mingled in with the mess in the bowl as Daniel fell back exhausted and feeling worse than he ever had in his life.

"Get him to the infirmary," Sloane said in his unexcited way of speaking. "Keep him under guard though and don't underestimate him. He may look sick but what we just did to him, won't kill him," he paused one of his melodramatic pauses, "and if it does, well, then we'll be wrong."

The bowl had the lid flipped shut and locked then it was carried at arm's length to the Pentagon laboratory for full investigation.

When Daniel woke half an hour later, Sloane was standing in front of him, watching with those piercing green eyes.

Daniel felt pretty good really, except that he was extremely hungry.

"Can I eat now," he said his voice sounding light and strangely foreign.

"Sure what would you like?" Sloane asked his arms crossed over his dark blue suit.

"You're psychic, you tell me," Daniel managed a chuckle. He didn't feel sorry that the alien was removed, in fact he felt grateful.

"I lied. I don't really have any special powers, not like you do."

"Me, what do I have?"

"Well let's see, your stomach lining re-grew in less than twenty minutes."

"Don't remind me of that," Daniel squirmed on the bed and found he was wearing handcuffs on his ankles and wrists.

"You know I am with the FBI, I can be trusted."

"Maybe," Sloane said "I'm sure you could free yourself if you wanted to."

Daniel looked at him with some contempt and pulled his wrists away from the bed, the handcuffs broke. He sat up in bed breaking the restraints on his feet. Sloane watched passively.

"Cartier has the ability to heal himself instantly, almost before he is hurt you know."

"Yes, I know that," Daniel said. "The creature told me a lot of things."

"I know it did, that was why we let you keep it within you as long as we did. However, we eventually decided that it was time to remove it."

"I could have done that myself with a lot less pain," Daniel said.

"Yes, you thought you could, but I don't think it would have left willingly."

"It told me of another race that are here. A race that could be allies to us."

"Or another enemy," Sloane finished and then waited as a soldier came in with some food, an egg salad sandwich. "It's free range," he said with the hint of a smile.

Daniel took the sandwich, removed the egg and ate it quickly, then he ate three more.

"You've lost some weight these last few days, you need to build your strength up again. I wasn't kidding about the Dead lands outfit."

"Aren't you worried that the creatures will know about that now," a sickening realisation dawned on him, the creatures knew everything he did, they had planted a spy within him which had pretended to be his friend.

"We had no reason to hide the Dead land plan. In fact we wanted them to know, perhaps it would make them leave our planet if they realize that we would rather destroy it than let them have it."

"How did you know I had one in me, if you're not psychic?"

"Let me show you something."

Sloane offered him a mini DVD player which Daniel took and pushed the play button.

It showed Daniel getting off the plane in Washington and being met by the men in black, Sloane was one of them. Daniel looked weak and his eyes were bloodshot but more than that, they were black. The pupil had completely taken oven the iris and the white.

"I'm surprised you didn't shoot me on sight," Daniel said.

"Well I wanted to" Sloane smiled. "Seriously we did all those tests on you, it was obvious that you had no knowledge of what you looked like, we made sure you didn't see a mirror until four days had gone by and then we let you shave, if you remember."

"Sure I remember, I looked okay then didn't I?"

"The DVD doesn't lie."

Daniel could see himself shaving, his skin was blotchy, purply and the eyes remained black. He had looked into a mirror and not seen any of it.

"What about the things it told me?"

"We don't know how much of that was true but we imagine it probably was. The creature could not help but allow you access to its mind. We don't know how much access it had in return but possibly a lot. We have already changed codes, moved people and done everything we think necessary to protect ourselves if all your knowledge has gone to the other side. Having said that, we don't think you knew much anyway, no offence."

"None taken," Daniel swung his legs off the bed and pulled the dangling cuffs off his wrists.

"You trust me completely?" He asked suddenly.

"More than you trust yourself right now," Sloane said.

"Do you have the creature?"

"We are trying to isolate it at this moment. Do you want to see it?"

"Sure, I have a few questions for it."

"Oh, okay, if you can still talk to it now it's out of your body."

Daniel saw his reflection in the mirror. He was thin, his eyes dull and his skin pallid. "I can talk to it from here."

Sloane peered at him from across the room. "If your eyes go black I may have to shoot you. Oh and talk out loud to it, I'd like to hear part of the conversation."

"No problem," Daniel said,. He looked in the mirror, his eyes looked normal and they remained that way to him throughout the next conversation.

"Where am I?" The creature asked

"You are in a bowl," Daniel responded.

"Why am I here? I want to be with you."

"You can't be with me anymore."

"Give me a host, let me live. I can help you.
"

"You were going to kill me."

"No, no! I was waiting until you were weak enough for me to become one with you. We need you Menarty."

"If I am Menarty, I don't need you and you can't infect me," Daniel said distantly, Sloane had to strain to hear him.

"Help me?"

"No, you're on your own."

The feeling of the creature's presence disappeared and Daniel looked at Sloane in the mirror. "Did my eyes go black."

"No, I can honestly say that they did not and I don't know if that's a good thing or a bad thing. How will we know if you are communicating with them now?"

Daniel swept his hair from his eyes, "I'll tell you."

"Good enough for me," Sloane said but his hand rested on his gun.

Chapter 13

Hatfield sat on the sand, his feet felt numb, he wanted to walk around, they had been kept here for the last two hours. Alex was standing in the middle of the arena, Caroline, Samantha and Richards had their backs against the wall, the creatures were over the other side.

"What's going on Alex?" Hatfield could stand it no longer, he was a soldier after all, he didn't want to die without putting up a fight.

"I don't know, they seem to be waiting for something. Are you vegetarian Colonel?

"No, I always liked a good steak myself. You think I'll become infected?"

"I don't know, I have a feeling that as they become more human they need to do a bit more than just bleed on you to infect."

"I bet they have to bite you," Caroline whispered, her eyes filled up with tears again. She was so frightened she just wanted it to be over; she crawled forward before Samantha could stop her until she reached Alex in the middle. He sank to his heels and put his arm around her, the creatures watched with hungry eyes.

"Not food" they all said in unison.

A loud rumbling noise seemed to come from all around them and the wall nearest the glass started to move revealing a door and some steps.

"Oh brilliant," Richards said as he stood up and pulled Samantha to her feet.

"You had a way out all the time and you didn't mention it?" Alex rounded on Richards.

"Gee, we'd have to be pretty stupid not to have a way down here wouldn't we?"

Alex wanted to rip his head off and was suddenly aware of Tim moving forward. He put his hand up so that Tim would not pass.

Tim stopped and looked puzzled, he indicated Richards with his eyes, he had heard Alex's thoughts and wanted to carry them out for him.

Alex guessed what had happened and shook his head. "No, only me," he said to Tim.

Tim smiled, all the creatures smiled and he moved back to join them, they liked their new leader's plan. They had been worried that they couldn't understand his mind but it appeared to be just a glitch, he was like them. He wanted to rip someone's head off too.

The door in the wall stood open and a creature like the advanced ones moved forward. It stepped to the side and indicated that all of the occupants of the arena were to leave by that door. Steps led immediately upwards.

"Where does it lead to?" Alex asked, throwing a glance at Richards. The man's eyes were full of hostility.

"Where does it go?!" Hatfield demanded.

Richards relented. "Back up to the main lab, the other side of the glass where all the creatures are. It comes out in the freezer, hope they have it turned off."

"I'll go first," Alex said.

"No!" Caroline cried.

"She's right, we don't want to be stranded with these things, you'd better go last, I'll lead the way," Hatfield commanded. At least now he felt they had a chance.

Samantha and Richards followed Hatfield, with Caroline and Alex next, then Tim and his friend. They made a long procession moving up the stone steps to come out in the freezer room. To their relief, the freezer was turned off.

The most striking thing about the freezer room was that everything had been removed from it. There were no bodies of any kind. Someone had furnished it with beds and chairs.

Tim and his friends left the freezer room and closed the door behind them, and the door down to the arena automatically locked.

"So now we're in a new prison," Samantha moaned.

"At least we're alive," Hatfield said.

"I wonder what sort of torture your friends used to find out about the secret door?" Richards said

"They don't need to use torture, they just turn one of the scientists and all his knowledge goes with them. That's how they work. That's why they're looking more human. I think they may have the ability to change the way they look. Eventually, when they have evolved enough, we won't know who to trust," Alex lay down on a bed.

"I think we know who we can't trust," Richards said.

Alex swung his legs back over the side of the bed "Are you suggesting that you can't trust me, even now?"

Richards almost laughed and looked away.

"We all heard you speak to that creature Alex. You said only me. What did you mean by that?" Samantha asked.

"I," this was not going to sound so good Alex realized. "It doesn't matter what the thing thought I was saying."

"Tim." Hatfield reminded him, "You called it Tim."

"What? Now you don't trust me either?"

"Nobody trusts you," Richards said.

"I do," Caroline said and went to his side.

"I do to, surprisingly," Samantha said, "Certainly more than I trust you Seth."

"Samantha!" Seth Richards felt a spasm of jealousy cut through him.

"You seem to forget that you had me imprisoned, Caroline was made to be a guinea pig of some sort and who knows what you did to Alex in the early days when you kept us away. For all I know you may have made him the way he is now."

"The way I am now?" Alex asked

"You're different. There use to be a kind of gentleness about you, a caring side that seems to have vanished."

"I still care'; Alex said coldly, "Just not about the same things," he lay back down on the bed. "Now if you don't mind I'd like to get some sleep."

"Sleep! You can sleep now?" Samantha asked her voice rising.

"He's right," Hatfield said, "we should all take the opportunity to sleep. Who knows what is going to happen, or why they've kept us here or where anybody else is."

"Dead probably," Seth said.

"Maybe," Alex said quietly from his bunk.

Alex tried to sleep but he couldn't shut out the other's voices, they were still talking about him and his relationship to the monsters. They feared him, even Samantha was not as sure as she had been and then after Hatfield had lay down to take a nap and Caroline had curled up under a bunk, he could still hear Samantha talking to Richards and it ground into his very being. Mustn't think bad thoughts or the creatures will come and take him away, he thought.

"You know I still care about you a great deal. We were about to get married once you know," Richards said.

"I know but you're, well we split up didn't we? We stopped seeing each other before Alex showed up."

"No, actually we drifted apart as soon as Alex showed up," Richards said.

"Seth, I didn't leave you, I didn't stop seeing you."

"No, I guess it was me that instigated the whole thing. I was so caught up in what was happening, I didn't have time for you. As for Cartier."

"You became more obsessed with him than you ever were with me."

"He could still be our only hope," Richards conceded and Alex felt a wave of pride ripple over him. "Promise me you'll kill me if I become one of them, and I'll do the same for you."

"Thanks," Samantha said without any conviction.

Richards stroked her cheek and turned her face towards him. "I still love you Samantha."

Alex did not want to hear this, why don't they just come and take him away, he thought.

The talking had stopped, Alex opened his eyes and looked across at them, they were kissing. Just a small impassioned kiss but it was enough. He hated them both, what could she see in Richards anyway? Alex thought he was better looking, okay so Richards was fairly young to be in such a powerful position and had some classical good looks about him, but who wanted that these days. He was able to protect her from these monsters far better and also he couldn't be killed, Richards could be killed mutilated, eaten, turned into one of them and who knows what else. He closed his eyes again and listened.

"Don't Seth. It's too late for us now," Samantha whispered. "Besides, how can you be with me when you have the world to save?"

That did make Alex's skin prickle, he was the one who could save the world not Richards. You're behaving like an idiot Alex said to himself, oh great, now I'm talking to myself.

"As they get more human I think they can hear what Alex is thinking. As soon as they work out that he's not on their side, then we're in trouble" Samantha was saying.

"Sure he's on our side?" Richards snorted.

"Yes I am. He has every reason in the world to hate you anyway after what you've done to him and Caroline. You know that."

"Every reason? If only he did have," Richards said.

The door made a noise and swung open, more light poured into the room, two creatures of the older variety with matching drool stood at the open door. One of them indicated Richards. There were more of them outside. Tim made his way through and spoke, "Come," it said.

"What, come where?" Richards asked

Tim glanced at Alex with a flicker of his eyes. Alex sighed and made his way over.

"No, not food." he pointed at Richards.

"We know," Tim said, there was a new intelligence in his eyes, he still couldn't get Alex's thoughts. It perplexed him. He heard Alex less than an hour a go, they all had. He had wanted them to remove this man and kill him, now he was not sure they had interpreted correctly.

"You wanted us to take him," Tim said, his tongue finding the words slowly.

Alex felt his face flush and the eyes of the others upon him.

"No, I never said that."

Tim shook his head and walked up to Alex, he looked deep into his eyes and saw only a stone wall looking back.

"But I heard you?" He said unsure whether he had.

"Where are the others?" Alex asked changing the subject.

"They are locked up, they are for eating and for turning," Tim looked at Caroline. "Not food," he said.

"Yes, yes okay. Can't you eat anything but people?"

"Not yet, but we will some day," Tim said.

"Why don't you put all the prisoners in here rather than keeping them in different places? Then we can see who is left." Alex said

"You want all in here? Too many, could put people for turning in, would please?" Tim's tongue was showing through his lips, it betrayed his pleasure at doing something to please Alex.

"Yes. Would please," Alex responded.

The other creatures grabbed Richards and started to carry him away. Caroline screamed.

Alex rushed over and pulled one off, the other raised its clawed hand to him but Tim let out a roar and it backed off.

Tim walked over and looked at Richards then at Alex.

"Perhaps we did not understand."

"He needs medical treatment, so does Hatfield," Alex said.

"Need doctor?" Tim asked.

"Yes, need doctor," Alex replied.

Tim nodded and left, the other creatures followed. Richards moved away from Alex and sat down, his leg had started to bleed again.

"Why did they think they heard you?" Samantha asked, "what could have caused that?"

"They did hear me," Alex confessed. "If I think something with enough emotion they can obviously pick it up. I don't know how long it will be before they can read my mind completely."

"They might never be able to," Richards said, " as long as you don't send out powerful messages to them like getting rid of people you don't like."

"Look I had no idea they could pick up on anything I thought. I saved you again didn't I?" Alex looked over to Samantha. If she doubted him anymore he would be lost.

"This time," Richards said.

The firing of bullets could be heard outside in the laboratory, there was also screaming and strange squeals like mice faced with the prospect of fighting giant cats. The door flew open and six soldiers stood there, their weapons pointed towards the occupants of the room.

"Hold your fire," Hatfield shouted.

"Major Hatfield, sir! We thought that you were dead. We waited for our chance and then took out about half a dozen of them. We managed to get a message off to HQ and they're sending a helicopter. We're to make our way to the roof sir. The lift is working again"

"Well done men," Hatfield looked at Richards, "that man is under military guard, as soon as we're out of here, I want him under close arrest."

"Yes, sir."

Hatfield, Samantha and Richards moved forward and joined the soldiers; spare weapons were handed to them. Alex remained where he was with Caroline.

"Come on man, we've got to get out of here," Hatfield said looking back.

"With them?" Alex asked.

"Sir, we have to go!" The soldiers became more agitated as noises could be heard along the corridor.

"Wait a moment," Hatfield went back to Alex. "What is the problem?"

"Don't you think it a bit strange that just these six made it? Where are all the others? How many were there down here, twenty, thirty?"

"More like fifty. What's your point? We have to get out and let HQ know that this facility is compromised and also what we are up against."

"I don't trust them. How do we know that they are not infected? This could be just a trick to infiltrate other places that they have not been able to get into. We don't know how it spreads or who's immune completely."

"I agree with him," Richards stood behind.

"I don't want to hear anything you have to say. As far as I'm concerned I'd rather leave you behind," Hatfield said.

"Let's go sir!"

"We don't have a choice; we have to get out of here. If they have signalled for a helicopter, I'm sure they'll show their hand before it gets here. Now let's go. What are your choices anyway?"

"I'm going to stay," Alex said. He let go of Caroline's hand and pushed her towards Hatfield. "Take Caroline with you and keep her safe."

"No! I won't go with them; I have to stay with you."

"Go with Samantha."

"I'm staying too," Samantha said.

"We haven't got time for a debate sir," the soldier interjected.

"I can't let you stay," Hatfield raised his gun and pointed at Alex. "You are too important to us and could be too important to them."

Alex pushed Caroline towards Samantha.

"You're just going to have to shoot me then. I have to stay to find out what's going on. I can probably get out on my own. If I'm on my own."

"You won't know where we are. The new HQ is a secret and secure location. You would never find it."

"Let's hope you're right. Samantha, take Caroline and go with them. This is your best chance to get out."

Samantha took Caroline's hand and pulled her away, she didn't look back, she didn't want him to see the tears of anger in her eyes.

"You'll be all right Caroline," he called after them.

"Do you want me to leave Richards with you?" Hatfield asked as he lowered his weapon.

"No, definitely not," Alex said.

"Thanks," Richards said, "in high demand as usual." He caught a look from Alex, a look that said, look out for them.

Alex moved into the laboratory and watched them go. He wondered if he should have kept Samantha and Caroline with him. Weren't they safest with him? He knew that the Hatfield would order a missile strike on this location as soon as he was able. They all knew that. So why hadn't he gone with them? He didn't know. Something had told him not to go. Then it struck him, the creatures had placed the desire to stay within him, the creatures knew the others were leaving and wanted them to. His initial feelings had been correct. The men had been compromised.

He ran after them and tried to catch them before they reached the lift. All the time he kept thinking, don't hurt Samantha or Caroline, not food, not food, not food. Why didn't I go with them? He should have gone with them to the surface and then split up from Hatfield and the others with just Sam and Caroline. He hoped he could catch up with them, he turned a corner and fell over something on the ground, it was a dead creatures body, its head torn off. He tried to clamber to his feet to catch up with them and was hit on the head from behind, a big blow that would have killed most men and left him unconscious on the floor.

They reached the elevator, it was waiting there, no creatures were around. As they were about to get on Samantha noticed some blood on the wrist of one of the soldiers.

"Are you wounded?" she asked.

"No, it's a bite mark, I don't know where it came from," the soldier replied, his eyes flashed as he realized what she was thinking. He glanced nervously at the others.

Samantha took off down the corridor back towards Alex, dragging Caroline behind her. She was not going with them, her best chances were with Alex. Seth's voice echoed after her but the others were already on the elevator and they were not pursuing her, they wanted to get to the roof, a helicopter and the goal of their mission.

Hatfield pulled Seth back into the elevator. "She may be better off with him. We need to warn the outside world and impart what we know and you seem to be the most qualified to do that, besides the helicopter won't wait."

The elevator doors closed and Seth found himself at the point of a gun with probably infected guards and a hostile commander. He wondered who they would find in charge at HQ, the British, the Americans or the creatures, either way he was in trouble.

Samantha kept running with Caroline at her side until she reached the corridor that led to the East side of the complex where Alex had stayed. Before this corridor had been empty, now it was crawling with creatures. They moved slowly towards her. Some of them were down on all fours, their necks craned up to look into her eyes. Caroline's hand trembled in hers as the horde surrounded them.

She could hear them chanting, "not food, not food, not food," and every now and then she heard somewhere a few of them were saying, "hungry, very hungry."

Chapter 14

Seth Richards had been a loner most of his life. His childhood had been remarkable for the fact that he survived it. The beating he took from his father stopped when he was fifteen when he had taken a kitchen knife from the drawer and pushed it through his father's heart. His mother had come home that night to find herself a widow and her son removed into care. The hearing was short, everyone knew his father, the uncontrollable fits of violence that accompanied his drinking, his record for violence against his wife and son for the past twelve years or so. The panel people were convinced that the killing of one Dwain Richards was a matter of self defence and praised the lad accordingly. Although at that time Seth was scrawny and ill nourished, everyone in the small American town was a little pleased that he had somehow got the better of his muscular and far stronger father.

Seth had always been bright, though he had never had a chance to excel at anything as any enthusiasm had been soon crushed by his parents. He didn't blame his mother, Lisa, she had just wanted a quiet life and was afraid that Seth's accomplishments would make his father feel inadequate. Lisa Richards had come from a well to do family in the South. She had gone on a tour of the country at the age of twenty with some friends, met Dwain, married him and never returned home. She had cut her parents out of her life as Dwain had requested and gone from rich spoilt girl to poor white trash in one swift movement. By the time she found out about the real Dwain, it was too late, she feared for her life and had no-where to turn, plus she was pregnant. After Seth was born, her parents called and wanted to see him. She had agreed and secretly hoped that they would take her back into their lives and help her make her escape before it was too late. Unfortunately her parents were killed in a car crash on their way to see her, only five miles from the small house where she waited for them clinging onto her son with new hope. Under Dwain's influence she had said some nasty things to her parents, had tried to hurt them as much as possible and had told them that she never wanted to be part of their family again. Her mind had been corrupted by drugs, supplied to Dwain as a favour for letting his new pretty wife sleep around with a few of his so called friends. That had stopped when she had reached her fifth month of pregnancy. Now she was afraid that if she stayed with Dwain, it would all start again.

When she heard the news of her parent's death, a large part of her died inside. She hadn't seen them for two years but had loved them dearly. As their only child, they had been heartbroken when she left and had tried many times in the first few months to talk to her, but Dwain had always managed to control everything and kept them at bay.

So hurt had her parents been by her behaviour that they had cut her out of the will and left the whole amount to a dog refuge. Dwain was very unhappy about it, shouting, kicking and swearing at all hours of the day for months. Lisa didn't care, her life was over and only the love of her child stopped her from taking her own life.

The night before Seth killed his father, the three of them had gone out to a nice restaurant. They had acted like a real family, for some reason Dwain was happy, he let them order whatever they wanted. He told them not to worry about the money, he had a job lined up. Seth never really knew what he did; it seemed to change from one day to the next.

The next afternoon Seth found his mother crying in the bedroom. He only stayed around for her, he would have left many times if it was not for the fear that he would never see her again. Many times she had put herself in harm's way to protect him. Lisa told him that she had to go out with a friend of daddies, that she would be home late. Then she told him about her early drug introduction and that sometimes Dwain used her to get things he wanted from his redneck friends. Once Dwain had ordered her to get into a strange van and lie in the back with her eyes blindfolded and her arms tied behind her. Eventually a man got in and took her clothes off, then he had sex with her twice. Dwain had been given a new lawn mower for that little scenario. She told Seth about her parents death and how Dwain had taunted her years later, when he had been drunk that his friends had arranged the little accident for her parents. Not only that but that she had paid for it herself by sleeping with them the night before. She had wondered what Dwain would get for that episode, when she spent the night with five men in an old barn, they had given her a lot of alcohol and threatened to tell her husband if she did not do all that they asked. She should have known that he had set it up. Suddenly she realized that everything had poured out, that her fifteen year old son had heard everything that was bad and sordid about her, that he now knew the extent of his father's evil soul. He had stood looking at her for some time and then left the room. He did not know what to say to her.

He heard her go out to rendezvous with whoever it was that had paid for their meal the previous night and heard his father come in. Seth walked into the sitting room where his father had sat down to watch television. He sat next to him, Dwain was in a good mood and they shared a father, son quality time watching some action thriller on the small screen. At the end, Dwain got himself a few cans of beer and offered one to Seth. Seth politely refused and excused himself. He went into the kitchen and sat there for nearly an hour, wondering how he could go through life with the knowledge he now held. He opened the kitchen drawer and took out the long sharp carving knife. He went back into the sitting room, his father was asleep on the settee. Seth plunged the knife into his chest and held it there while Dwain thrashed and tried to knock him off.

Seth thought about that now as he was being led to certain death by these human lookalikes that were almost certainly about to become flesh eating monsters. The memory had been repressed for so long, he had convinced himself that he had killed his father in self defence, that his mother had been a picture of virtue and that his childhood had been forgotten, not because it was so bad but because it was just unmemorable. Now the revelations had hit him hard, his stress level climbed to his brain and pierced it with a jagged edge and Seth Richards was locked in his own mind.

He had excelled at school after the death of his father and had eventually joined the CIA, from that he had had a couple of experiences that had made him a good candidate for the FSS (federation of special services). Being a member of this organization meant that you were highly trained, intelligent, probably with a degree, though Seth did not have one, but he would not hesitate to order a kill or carry one out if it was deemed necessary. He had not come all this way to be eaten by some monster that had low communication skills.

He knew he had made an enemy out of Alex Cartier, which had probably not been wise but the complication of Samantha had clouded his mind. He wanted to go back for her, true, he did not really care about Caroline or the others but he loved Samantha. Considering the traits of his father and how unlike him he was, it seemed likely that someone else had been his father entirely. Of this he was sure and would confirm it with his mother when he returned to the US, if she was still alive.

"Richards!" Hatfield was shouting at him.

"What!"

"I thought something was wrong with you, you just went off into a dream."

"You thought it necessary to wake me and bring me back to this, gee thanks," the flippant remark was hollow and sounded as though it came from outside his body. His eye twitched, his mouth as dry as a man without saliva glands.

The doors opened and the soldiers jumped out, their weapons ready but the lobby was empty, Seth was not surprised. He glanced towards the revolving doors that led to the outside world and wondered he stood any more chance out there.

"Let's go!" Markise, the loud soldier was shouting again, Seth found himself pushed along with the others as they made their way up the stairs to the top of Centre Point. He was sure they could have taken the elevator, after all, the creatures wanted them to get away didn't they?

"Hatfield, let me have a weapon, just in case, you know I'm on your side," Seth said, he was fairly sure that the major had not been compromised. Seth thought back to his father, his childhood, his head ached, he was having a bad time staying in the real world.

The helicopter arrived and the soldiers looked up towards it with black eyes.

Seth pushed into one of them and grabbed the sub automatic from them. Hatfield was too shocked to know what to do or whether to shoot. The helicopter landed to their right as Seth opened fire on the six soldiers and killed them before they had a chance to point their guns. Hatfield pulled his hand gun and shot Seth in the back, he fell on top of a dead soldier and their blood mingled. Hatfield went over to him to shoot him in the head, "you maniac, these are my men, you maniac!" He pointed the gun at his head.

People from the helicopter called him and he went over to them, shooting Seth was too good for him, he thought, let the creatures eat him alive.

"Colonel, are your all right?" The pilot asked, "What just happened, is that man dead?"

"Let's get out of here," Hatfield replied, "we can't help those men now." He sank into the seat of the helicopter and watched the building get further away as he was carried somewhere in Norfolk to the secret emergency base. He mourned the loss of his soldiers, men under his command, and more than that he had heard their thoughts as they died. He had linked to their minds and something buried deep within him had been activated. He just hoped that it wouldn't show until he reached his destination.

Seth lie on top of the dead bodies, he pushed himself off and tried to clean away their blood from his hands and face. The bullet in his back had missed his vital organs but the pain forced him to stop moving and watch, helplessly as the helicopter flew away. He knew he should have killed Hatfield as well, he should even kill himself. He sighed deeply and a pain shot through him like ice. He laughed and felt several more spasms until he could laugh no more and the tears rolled down his face. He knew that some of the soldiers blood had gone in his mouth. If any had been consumed he knew that he would be infected. He tried to reach for the submachine gun and found he couldn't, his whole body had become paralysed. He lay there waiting, either for death or for the creature process to happen and deep down, a new process was happening, his mind was coming to terms with everything that had happened in his life and a new Seth Richards was mentally being reborn and as he closed his eyes, the old Seth was no more.

Chapter 15

Samantha held Caroline tightly as the creatures advanced towards them.

"Not food, not food," they kept saying, their tongues clicking every now and then as they swallowed large amounts of drool, though some spilled down their chins and grotesque humanesque faces.

"Hungry, hungry," the sound came from behind. Samantha wheeled around to find nine more creatures advancing on them. All of them were dressed in soldier's uniforms which were sometimes covered in blood and other stains.

Caroline sank to the floor dragging Samantha with her.

"Close your eyes," Samantha said and held Caroline so tightly she could hardly breathe.

The next second they were being lifted up , Samantha struck out, her hand caught by Alex as he pulled them both into him. Samantha almost fainted with pure relief, her arm went round his neck, he picked Caroline up with his other arm. Blood still dribbled down his right cheek onto caked blood from his angry head wound.

Confusion took hold of the creatures, they could see the one that was to be their leader, yet he was bleeding, they could smell his blood and it was not as they expected. He was foreign to them. Alex moved quickly forward while they awaited silent instructions on what to do. He pushed his way through them easily determined to get to the lift shaft.

"We're getting out of here," he whispered to Samantha and she knew then that she loved him.

As they reached the elevator shaft, more than a dozen creatures followed behind, Alex dabbed at the button to call the lift and wondered if they would allow them to leave.

There was obviously some kind of conversation going on between the creatures, they were arguing silently amongst themselves but the noise they generated in radio waves was intense. Caroline shivered at Alex's side as the elevator moved towards them. He still had his arm around Samantha and unconsciously pulled her closer to him. For a moment he glanced down at her and saw her beautiful eyes shining back filled with fear, hope and something more. He was about to speak to her and tell her it was all right when the monsters suddenly moved forward, they had received their orders not to let him leave.

The doors opened as the ghouls rushed forward, Alex just had time to push Samantha and Caroline into the elevator before they were upon him.

"Go!" He shouted as he was pulled back into the corridor.

Samantha had fallen against the side wall of the elevator; she reached up for the button and waited.

"Go!" he cried again as a creature bit down on his arm, Caroline screamed and sank back on the floor. Samantha pushed the button and the doors began to close.

Alex kicked one in the chest and sent it sprawling against some of the others, he whirled around kicking into one so hard that it split in two. Another sank its teeth into his shoulder down to the gums, he reached back and ripped its head off without a thought, then he leapt through the door of the elevator as it closed and started its journey back to the surface.

Samantha tried to throw her arms around him but he pushed her back.

"I'm contaminated; I have their slime and blood on me, stay away!"

"You can't be contaminated," Samantha responded as she fell on her arm.

Alex went to her side and helped her up, "I'm sorry I didn't mean to push you," he looked frightful. His face still covered in caked blood and now there was blood on his shoulder and arm.

"It's all right," she said and moved to Caroline who was still huddled in the corner.

Alex thought back to what he had just done, nine bodies lay dead below them. He had been as vicious and monster-like in his destruction of them as they had been themselves. He wondered if the carnage had been relayed to all the other creatures of the world and whether they would still consider him their leader, he thought not.

The elevator doors opened at ground level and cautiously they left the safety of the small iron box and glanced furtively around the lobby area. It was devoid of any life and somehow more unnerving than if they had walked out to be greeted by a dozen creatures armed with submachine guns.

"There's a bathroom over there," Samantha said, "we could get out of this lobby area and plan our next move," her voice sounded quite steady apart from the waiver underneath it.

They made their way across the lobby and into the bathroom area. Alex caught sight of himself in the mirror and recoiled. He smashed a towel machine open and ripped some off the drum.

Samantha and Caroline both jumped and eyed him with some apprehension.

"I need to go," Caroline said.

"Go where?" Samantha asked.

Caroline glanced towards the stalls.

"Oh, sure, me to," Samantha glanced at Alex as he washed the blood from his face.

Luckily once he had washed there seemed very little injury on him. The head wound was almost completely healed which he had received from the unknown assailant. The bites had already started to close and once the blood was off his face, he was almost his old handsome self again. Samantha was now by his side and made a movement with her hand towards his head. He caught her wrist and she let out a cry of alarm rather than pain. He realized she held a towel in her hand and was merely about to examine the head wound and let her go.

"I'm sorry," he said, "I" he looked into her eyes and saw fear, sadness and that something he had seen before.

"How did you get this?" she asked as she looked carefully at the healing gash in his head. "They would have had to hit you with a pointed bowling ball or something to get this kind of wound."

He took her wrist gently and moved it away from his head, "it still hurts," he said. "Someone hit me from behind or something."

"One of them?"

"I don't think so. It could have killed me."

"I doubt it," Samantha smiled.

"No, it could have killed me," Alex said firmly. "It could have kept hacking at me until I was in small pieces, but it didn't obviously." Alex realized he still held Samantha's wrist in his hand. Without thinking he pulled her to him and kissed her, the weeks of longing poured into that one kiss and he felt her respond with the same passion he kept in check.

"I love you," he said and the moment the words left his mouth he felt a great weight lifted from him.

Samantha was about to respond when Caroline moved into view.

"Where are we going now?" She asked her eyes large and soulful.

Alex released Samantha and she pushed his hair back. "I could do with a hair cut," he said as lightly as possible.

"A friend of mine has a flat near here, Sheldon Mansions just down the road, I have a key for it. We can stay there while we plan our next move. But first I need to go up to the roof and find out if there is anything we can use to communicate with the rest of the world and to see if there is any transport up there. You never know, a helicopter might be just waiting for us." He touched Caroline's face and she gave a wan smile.

"You're going to leave us here?" Samantha asked.

"Just for a few minutes."

"I think we should come with you," Samantha pleaded.

"Okay," he touched her hair with a stroking movement, he couldn't leave her alone.

"Let's go."

They made their way slowly but uneventfully to the top of Centrepoint and reached the helipad. Samantha knew of a hidden radio up there, underneath a stone slab. It was there for situations just like this. Only she knew of it and Colonel Hatfield, she hoped he had not taken it with him.

Alex saw the mound of bodies and then noticed a humming sound coming from them. He approached slowly noting who they were and that Hatfield was not there. Then he saw Seth, lying on his back in a contorted way and humming some jaunty number he couldn't quite place.

"Richards? Are you okay?" What a stupid question that was Alex thought as he bent down and saw the exit wound where the bullet had passed straight through the body.

"Hi there," Richard's voice was uplifted, trouble free and totally without reason.

"Any chance of a lift?" he giggled and tried to move, a spasm hit his body.

Samantha had rushed over, she held the radio by its cord.

"Seth, can you move?" Samantha took his hand.

"Come on baby light my fire," Seth sang.

Alex had started checking the weapons and had found a pistol plus ammunition; he also had a sub-machine gun and a rather sharp knife.

"We can't help him," Alex said trying to keep Caroline away. "Let's go. Why didn't you tell me about the radio?"

"I didn't think of it till we got here. We can call for help from here."

Alex knelt down and touched Samantha's arm. "We can't help him. He is contaminated and also paralysed plus he seems to be having some sort of breakdown."

"You can't just leave him," Samantha said her eyes flashed angrily.

"I'll do exactly what he would do in the circumstances," Alex replied coldly.

"No! I won't let you kill him."

"He's already dead," Alex said as he prepared the pistol.

"Whoa, beg to differ there old chap." Seth's body seemed to move of its own accord and he suddenly found himself sitting up. The paralysis was gone and the wound had already started to heal.

Alex pointed the pistol at him, "he's one of them, Sam, I have to take him out now before he progresses to the next stage."

"He's not one of them," Caroline said as Seth hummed on, "he's something else."

Alex couldn't shoot him in front of the others, not unless he looked dangerous and he certainly didn't. There was a calmness about him that did not exist around the others. An innocence that belonged to a newly born child not a hardened ex CIA man or brain-eating monster.

Alex pulled Caroline and Samantha back as Seth stood up. He looked at them with questioning eyes and smiled. His tongue was playing around his teeth, they were growing, changing, getting sharper. The others looked on with growing horror.

His fingernails began to grow quickly and became talons as he watched them.

"Going to make it hard to bite my nails now," he said with a slight grin.

"So what's going on?" he asked with his sharp jagged teeth, taloned hands and blackish eyes.

Alex wanted to just lift the gun and shoot him but he knew that Samantha would never have forgiven him if he had.

"Do you know who you are?" Samantha asked taking a step towards him. Alex immediately pulled her back.

"Sure my name is ," he hesitated and his eyes cleared back to their blue colour "Frankenstein. Yeah Frankenstein and you're Gilda, he's Zorro and the little one," he indicated Caroline with a taloned finger, "she's Dorothy."

"Oh brother," Alex said as he let out a large sigh. "He's contaminated but his mind's gone. They probably can't reach him, he has undergone the physical change but he still appears to be on our side. It may be best if we just shoot him."

"No," the girls resounded in unison.

"Seth we are going to try to get help" Samantha said

"Who's Seth?" Seth replied.

"I meant Frank."

"Okay, what's happening at the moment? Are we in Kansas?" Frank asked.

"We can't trust him," Alex said pointedly.

"Seth, don't you remember me?" Samantha asked with such fondness that Alex was tempted to pull the trigger and face the consequences after.

"Course, the monster Frankenstein created didn't really have a name but you just can't call me monster so I thought, Frankenstein would be okay and hey, well, why not just make it Frank."

"Are you a monster?" Caroline asked.

"One I created myself I think with the help of some creature gloop, ingested no doubt, yuk!"

"I think we can trust him," Samantha snapped, "the break from reality although disconcerting, is not complete, he still knows what is going on, so we just need to make sure he knows what side he is on." Samantha tried to move towards Frank again but Alex still restrained her.

"Supposing he bites you? I don't want to lose you, I don't want to take that chance."

"Rita, I do remember you and Dorothy and the tin man, oh no he's not here, oh well. Who were you again?" Frank looked at Alex and pointed one of his taloned fingers.

"Zorro," Alex shook his head.

"Well okay, let's go kick some ass."

"Anybody's in particular?" Alex asked.

"Nah, you point and I'll kick," Frank beamed.

"The radio isn't getting any response," Samantha chipped in as she flipped the dial.

"Perhaps there isn't anyone there to respond," Alex said. "We'll go via my friend's flat down the road, see if she's still alive, then we'll head out to an airport."

"Which airport?" Samantha asked

"Stansted would be a good bet I would think. I took some lessons there once, we can at least use one of the planes to get us around the country and see where the human stronghold is. If it is."

"Airport, da, da ,da smiling face, you took the ghoul I love so far away, fly her away, mind that large tray," Frank sang. The sudden loud noise made the other three leap out of their skin.

Alex looked at Samantha and she shook her head, they could not kill him, she was sure that he was very important to them and he was still Seth to her.

"Keep the noise down Frank," Alex accentuated the Frank part.

"Oh, right. Sorry. Dum, dum dum dum," Frank continued to sing and tried to click his fingers, but the talons just made a strange tapping noise.

"You won't be able to come with us if you make any noise," Samantha said looking into Frank's eyes.

"Okay Gilda," Frank gave her a grotesque smile and continued to sing in his mind, his head bobbing from side to side, a happy aura around him. This was probably the happiest he'd ever been in his life.

They reached the lobby of Centrepoint, it was still deserted. Alex moved ahead and looked through the large doors. The street looked the same as last time he had been up here. The double decker bus still stood in the middle of the road. Other cars lay strewn about the area. There was no sign of any life.

Alex returned to the others, "Okay, we will go out the building and to the left, then just keep going until we reach Shelden Mansions, it's just a little way."

Frank put his hand over his mouth to stop another song from spilling out.

They reached the large double doors of Shelden without any hassle, the door was slightly ajar. Alex slowly pushed it open and entered into the gloominess, the others followed.

A large staircase was in front of them which wound its way up to the top of the building, there was a also a small quaint elevator which would have held three people at a crush. Frank sniffed around the elevator, " I'm not going in it," he said.

"That's fine," Alex replied, "we'll take the stairs."

"So who is this woman that we're about to break into her apartment."

"I use to have a key so technically we could pretend I'd lost it," Alex responded.

"Oh, a key. Sounds pretty serious," Samantha said softly.

"At the time it was," Alex continued to climb the stairs throwing sentences back over his shoulder. "I'm surprised you didn't know about her, she was with me the night I was bitten." He stopped and turned to face Samantha "Cassandra Stewart, ring any bells?"

"Oh, the woman you dreamt about. I'm sorry I should have thought about that. We don't know what happened to her, but this wasn't the address we had for her. It was somewhere in the country on an estate, I think."

"She was pretty well off, this was a secret flat she kept from her relations. I'm not even sure it was in her name. But if you didn't find any sign of her, then there's always the possibility that she could be alive and living here." Alex stopped and looked back at Samantha, she did not say anything. "I know what you're thinking, that the likelihood of her being alive is remote, that she was probably eaten alive."

"I'm not saying anything," Samantha said quietly. She could tell that this woman had meant a great deal to Alex at one time. After all, he was still dreaming about her.

Frank flung his hand over his mouth and mumbled something through it, no-one took any notice.

They reached the flat, the door was closed, Alex knocked lightly on it, then a bit harder. He turned and smiled at the others and then kicked it suddenly with little force, it flew open.

The room looked untouched, everything was in its place, the sunlight fell through the large windows of the lounge bathing everything in a warm glow.

Caroline sank down onto the couch and closed her eyes, within moments she was asleep. Samantha sat next to her beckoned to Frank to sit on the opposite chair, he did so willingly.

Alex checked the bathroom and the kitchen then he went into the main bedroom. The curtains were drawn and the room remained in darkness apart from where the light fell in from the hallway.

Alex stared at the bed, something was there, he could see the outline of a woman sitting upright on the bed. His eyes adapted with a jolt, it was if light had filtered through every corner of the room and he saw Cassandra sitting there, staring straight ahead, her eyes glassy, her mouth closed, her arms folded in her lap before her.

Alex flicked the light switch and took a step into the room.

Cassandra's eyes sprang to life and she turned her head with a sharp movement towards him, a shiver took hold of his spine.

"Hello darling, I've been waiting," it said.

Chapter 16

Alex froze in his tracks, the blood pumped round his body like an icy river curling its dead fingers against his warm skin. He closed the door behind him before the others became aware of their strange guest, he stared at her in the harsh light of the bulb which had no cover.

Her skin looked stretched and pallid, her mouth partly open and her tongue would dart out occasionally. He knew that his Cassandra was gone and yet he longed to believe that there could be something of her left inside, something he could bring back.

She let out a short sigh and swung her legs round off the bed, her head movements were jerky like a puppet being worked by a beginner. Her arms raised up towards him, she smiled and her teeth looked normal, she was not one of them, this was something new.

"We see you," she said her voice much lower than usual, "we're coming for you."

Alex backed up to the door, opened it and jumped back into the hallway, a hand touched his shoulder and he wheeled round.

"Sorry, I didn't mean to make you jump," Samantha said as she noted his wide-eyed expression.

"I, it's not polite to sneak up," Alex stammered keeping his hand on the door knob.

"Anything in there?" Samantha asked in a way that said she knew there was.

"Old girlfriend, turned into some sort of zombie, I would think," Alex opened the door and peaked in, he closed it again quickly.

"Yep, she's a zombie all right."

"One of them?" Samantha asked

"No," a vicious ripple ran down his back, "something else."

"May I look? You could be just wanting to see her."

"I don't think that I'd want to see her like that," Alex replied tightening his grip on the door handle in case it was wrenched from his hand at any second.

Samantha slid her hand over his, the touch made him loosen his grip and he felt his palm tingle. "Let me look," she said "you could be concussed, you still have a nasty bump on your head from whatever hit you and you need to rest. We hit you with all sorts of things and couldn't create a bump like that. Besides if she is something else, she might be like Seth, I mean Frank, an ally."

Alex hesitated for a moment and then turned the doorknob and looked in towards the bed, it was empty. He pushed the door open and stared at the place where Cassandra had been sitting. Well, the indentation was there.

Samantha peered past him, "See, there's no-one here." She pushed by and walked into the room before he could grab her arm. The door slammed shut behind her and she was faced with Cassandra's vacant face staring at her from behind the door.

Alex frantically tried to open the door again but it would not move, even with all his strength he could not budge it.

"Oh my, what have we here?" the monster said loudly on the other side of the door, "a tasty morsel that my love has sent to me." She started to advance towards Samantha.

"Alex! Alex," Samantha cried out as she backed away from the jerky puppet on invisible strings that opened its mouth in anticipation of the meal to follow.

"I won't hurt you," it said, "I just want to taste your insides."

"Alex get in here," Samantha screamed.

"I can't get the door open," Alex screamed back.

"It's just a wooden door," Samantha said, "there's nothing against it."

Alex pushed as hard as he could, he might as well have been pushing stone.

"What's happening?" Caroline asked.

"The door is stuck," Alex said. "Frank, help me open this door," Alex called back up the hall.

Frank ambled down and put his hand out towards the door, "You need to put a bit more into it than an outstretched hand," Alex spat under his breath.

"Um, there's nowhere to run in here, it's a very small room," a cracked voice echoed back. "

Alex," a sobbing sound followed.

Alex threw himself continuously against the door, "Help me, damn it."

"Not stuck," Frank said and stood back.

Alex turned to face him, "You get this door open or I will kill you."

"Not my fault," Frank pouted, "door will not budge. Energy is holding it. I can't help, not strong enough. You neither. Go through wall, quicker."

Samantha was backed against the far wall, Cassandra almost upon her. She held out her arm and the tip of her fingers touched Samantha's throat. Slowly she brought her other hand into view, along with the large butcher's knife she held in it. "I've been waiting for you," it said and lifted the knife, her eyes turned white and her throat gurgled.

Alex almost fell through the wall and knocked her way across the room, he had hit her so hard that her neck had stretched, barely hanging onto her head which was now at a right angle. She hit the wall and crumpled into a heap on the floor, the air knocked from her.

Samantha dropped into Alex's arms and they sank to the floor together. Caroline's scream had them scrambling to their feet as Cassandra stood up, her head lolled to the side and her steps were uneven, she still held the knife and started to advance towards them, Samantha moved behind Alex.

Cassandra slashed at the air as she got closer to them, Caroline screamed behind her. Cassandra's head turned to face behind her lolling on the broken neck, "I'll be with you in a minute my sweet," she said in her deep unnatural voice.

Alex lunged for the knife and pulled it from her grasp then he stabbed her where her heart should have been. She knocked him back against the wall so hard that he went halfway into the plaster then she pulled the knife from her chest. There was no blood.

"Now you've made a hole in my dress," it said as it twisted it's head to look down. It advanced on Samantha again.

Alex tried to get up but some force had him pinned against the wall. Cassandra glanced towards him as it decided who to kill first.

It decided on Samantha as Alex was powerless to prevent it but before it could reach her, Frank grabbed its flabby neck and twisted the head off, there was no blood. He picked up the still writhing body and threw it out of the window where it crashed to the street four stories below.

Alex felt the force leave him and he rushed to Samantha's side, Samantha was crying with a mixture of relief and fear. Caroline rushed to their side, the three of them in an embrace of devotion.

Frank watched them curiously, he picked up the lifeless head and chucked it over by the wardrobe, then he shrugged and threw his arms around the trio in a joint embrace that caused great feelings of alarm in Alex, yet they owed Frank their lives and could do nothing, for now.

"Okay, let's get out of here," Alex said as he extricated himself from the middle of the huddle.

"Yes, we must leave," Frank echoed, "there will be more of them, maybe."

"More of what?" Alex asked "Why couldn't I kill it, why couldn't I move, why didn't it bleed?"

"Uh, I seem to have forgotten," Frank said lightly. "What are we doing here?"

"Now you an amnesiac?" Alex pulled the others to their feet.

"Am I? Oh, are we going now? Must leave soon. We don't want them to find us."

"Oh for…" Alex moved back to the lounge area. "Why was I able to break through the wall and not the door?" He shook Frank hard enough to make his head jostle around.

"Alex! Let him go. He helped us, he saved us. He will tell us what he can when he can," Samantha pulled Frank free.

"It's probably looking for another dead body even now," Frank whined, "Let's go."

"Another dead body, it's still alive? What is it?" Alex gathered up their things.

"Downtown," Frank said.

"Downtown?" Alex was beginning to think he should just kill Frank as soon as possible.

"When you feel lonely and life is getting you lowly you can always go, down town," Frank sang.

"Not again. Don't sing, I'm warning you, don't sing," Alex grabbed Caroline's hand Samantha walked behind him and they made their way back down the stairs to the street. Frank followed behind singing softly under his breath, oblivious to everything and yet also very aware.

A new Volkswagen Polo had been abandoned not far from the building, the street looked deserted. Alex ran over to the car and jumped in, the keys were in the ignition, it started first time. He waved over to the others to join him.

"I used to have one of these," he said as they got in the car. "Very good for city driving, especially since we may need to do some pavement driving to get around the obstacles, though I doubt if it was tested on running over dead bodies."

"Where are we going?" Samantha asked.

"Maybe we should try Stapleford Abbots. I learnt to fly there. We may be able to get a plane working, then we can fly around the country looking for help, rather than being a moving target on the road"

"Is this car big enough? In case we pick up survivors on the way?"

"Big enough for two people, a child and a nondescript monster, I should say, plus a survivor if we come across one, plus the keys are in it and it isn't filled with dead bodies. Look I can only fly a small plane. We may not be able to all get in it" Alex looked directly at Frank.

"We can't leave him," Samantha said and opened the car door.

"Hop in the back Frank," She said.

"Weeeee." Frank said and made a big hop into the car. Caroline jumped in next to him.

Samantha sat next to Alex in the front, her face was dirty and she tried to clean it up with a tissue. Alex drove off avoiding other stationary vehicles and the occasional body parts. The remains of Cassandra's body had stopped moving though somewhere nearby, another body had been secured and was already securing a vehicle of its own to follow them.

Chapter 17

Alex had just got onto the motorway when Frank's face appeared in the rear view mirror, "want the door open."

"You can't have the door open while the car is moving," Alex finished the sentence under his breath, "not unless you were being dragged behind it with you arm caught on the latch."

"Alex!" Samantha looked at Frank and was suddenly uneasy at allowing him to sit next to Caroline in the back. "You must keep the door closed," she said as he started to try the door handle. Despite her warning Frank continued to try to open the door.

Alex whistled at the mirror and caught his attention, "Child locks are on, why don't you open the window if you need air."

"Okay," Frank seemed appeased, "Just need some air, no big deal Zorro. Don't want to be dragged by arm either."

Alex glanced guiltily at Samantha and saw a smile flicker across her face.

"What a strange little family we are," she said.

"Yes, two providers, one golden child and a creature that lives in never never land," Alex said and the two of them laughed. Caroline looked up in surprise, her face still drawn then she jumped as Frank started laughing. He looked quite grotesque, his mouth out of proportion with his teeth, he put his hand over his mouth as if he sensed how he must look. Alex and Samantha stopped as Frank carried on then Caroline started and they all laughed again more through relief at being alive than anything particularly funny.

"What a family," Frank said.

Alex had noticed the car in the rear view mirror, it was travelling some distance behind but it was definitely following them. He felt no presence from it, so the likelihood of it being one of his creatures seemed remote. Samantha had fallen asleep, her head angled towards him so that he could see her face. She looked so peaceful, but there was a slight sound coming from her chest and a tear rolled down a cheek.

"Maybe should wake her up, bad dream," Frank threw over from the back.

"Caroline sleep too , need to rejuvenate. You could sleep too if you want, I'll stay awake and watch the car following us."

Alex looked at him in the rear view mirror with some disdain, " Are you going to watch the other car from the back there?"

"Yes. Stay where I am," Frank lolled his tongue out like a huge dog and then quickly pulled it in again when he caught the look of revulsion on Alex's face.

"So I sleep, and you stay awake, watching from the back," Alex barely contained his contempt.

"Yes, that is what I said," a puzzled look appeared on Frank's face.

"And does the car drive itself while I'm sleeping or are you going to drive it from the back?"

Frank remained silent for a second then he turned his face to the window and called back, "Car probably not drive itself, we probably crash."

"That's what I thought," Alex glared at frank, he didn't trust him, he still thought it best to kill him but he wondered how much of that was because of who Frank was now or who Seth had been before.

Frank's eyes pierced into the rear view mirror.

"I can't see your soul," he said suddenly.

"Well, there's a blessing," Alex responded, though a chill had slipped along his back as fast as a grass snake taking cover from a lawn mower.

There was silence for a few minutes, the car following had not gained. Frank glanced back through the back window every now and then. Suddenly he threw himself up against the nearest door pushing his whole self away from Caroline. The movement made Alex almost jump out of his skin.

"What the hell's the matter now!" He said through gritted teeth not wanting to wake Samantha, even if she was dreaming about the end of the world.

"I don't want to be near it," Frank said and tried to push himself more into the door.

"Near what," Alex wanted to pull the car over, he was concerned at the way Frank was looking at Caroline.

"It," Frank repeated and then lapsed into silence.

The car had gained behind them and was starting to catch up.

The country road leading to Stapleford Abbotts was pretty deserted until they saw a car ahead with a shadow inside sat at the wheel. Alex was about to accelerate past when the door opened and a man got out. He waved at the them to stop.

Alex started to slow down, the car following also slowed, it did not want to catch them, yet. He felt no waves from this man, he had no connection and the man looked unharmed as he drove past.

The man held his fist in the air and shouted expletives at the car for not stopping, Alex pulled up twenty feet away and got out of the car. Samantha and Caroline had woken up.

"Stay here," Alex commanded with his most authoritative tone. The other car had stopped twenty feet on the other side. The man had seen both cars and was deciding which to walk towards.

"You think it's a survivor?" Samantha asked brushing her cheek with her hand. She must have realized that she'd been crying and was embarrassed by it.

"Not for long if the other car takes him. Frank get out the car, you're coming with me."

Frank shrugged, "Don't want to."

"Get out or I will shoot you," Alex said, his hand on a gun in his pocket.

"I'm coming." Frank leapt out of the car.

The stranger had started to move towards them but had stopped when he saw Frank. Even from where he stood he could see that there was obviously something wrong with him. He backed up and started to move towards the other car.

"Hey, it's all right," Alex shouted. "Wait here Frank."

"Wait, come, I don't know what to do," Frank sat down in the road. "I'll wait."

The other car door opened and figure stepped out and waved to the stranger. It stood waiting for the man to get to it, but he had stopped. Something about it had made Andrew Marn stop in his tracks.

Chapter 18

Andy was in his early forties, something of a tough guy. He had had his fair share of being bullied at school because of his weight and on leaving had turned his body into one mass of muscles. He had learnt various types of self-defence and had learnt boxing, eventually he had become a personal trainer to many of the richer people in the Essex and London area.

There were many women on his books whom he had trained and become close to. One of those was a Beth Palmer, a married forty year old with a flabby midriff and the need to be desired again. He had been with Beth, when everything had gone wrong with the world. They had seen on the news that such films as "Dawn of the Dead" appeared to be actually happening.

Beth was one of his richest clients and still fairly attractive. Many times he had thought of making a pass at her but the right time had not yet presented itself. She had been divorced about a year and her ex-husband still turned up on occasion. He was particularly glad he was with her now for she had something that no other woman he knew did, she had a high tech bomb shelter at the back of the house.

It had not taken much to convince her that the best place for them was in the shelter, just for a few days while the army took care of everything, as he had said they would. They had food, electricity, even television, there was enough space for four people. "It was designed for a family of four," she had said, a wistful look in her eye. "I couldn't have any more children after Safroni. It was why we broke up. You know my husband and I."

"Yeah. I know," Andy now had the perfect opportunity to get close to her. From that moment she had trusted him completely and allowed all her shortcomings and fears to pour out into his ever listening ear. On the third day together they made love and Andy knew that she was hooked on him. He may not have been terribly good-looking but there was a charisma about him that the women liked. On the fifth day Andy had taken stock of the rations in the bunker, according to the news, these zombie type creatures were proving difficult to kill. He concluded that there were enough rations for two people for about six months. Half of the store areas had not been stocked but he thought six months would probably be long enough before the army sorted out the man-eating monsters above. It was a very comfortable place. There was a big table for family dinners, a kitchen with microwave and tin opener, Six bunk beds, of which Andy moved two together to form a double. The place seemed to be made of stainless steel, except for the floor which was concrete base with a soft rubber paint on it and a couple of rugs for that home feeling. One wall contained six television screens which gave you a good view of the hatch and the surrounding area. Unfortunately there was no sound so although you could see the birds singing, you were unable to listen to their harmonic tones.

They had a two way radio and had communicated several times with other people with two way radios, though their communication stopped on the fifth day when the airways went quite. On the sixth day her ex husband turned up. Although the bomb shelter had a locking hatch, it also had an intercom system which allowed you to speak and see someone on the outside. Her husband looked frantic, filthy and there was blood caked on his head around the temple. Andy had been sleeping when Graham had arrived, had he been awake, maybe the following murder and mayhem would not have taken place.

Beth had opened the lock and allowed Graham to climb down, he had a girl with him whom she hadn't seen on the viewer, he had kept her out of sight. Andy woke with a start, feeling something was wrong, he rushed over to the hatch only to find they now had company.

"What's he doing here?" Graham had asked as he wiped the blood from his head," He hadn't waited for an answer just pushed by to find himself some clean clothes.

"I'm Cleo," the girl looked about eighteen. She sensed them staring at her. "Graham saved me from some horrible creatures."

Andy saw little point in reprimanding Beth for letting them in, after all it was done. The hatch had a security code to open it. Beth had told him all about it when they had first gone down there. He even knew how to reprogram it, or thought he did, that way he was sure no other unwelcome guests would arrive and eat his food. Unfortunately, he didn't know how to reprogram it properly and in trying to change the code he had caused it to reset to the manufacturer's setting, a point that he would not be aware of until two days later.

After cleaning up, Graham told them about the riots above, the strange creatures and how they killed. At first it seemed random, massacres of everyone they came across but then according to news reports, some people were being spared. It was as though the creatures were looking for someone. All the time the numbers were increasing, if someone didn't die, they turned into a monster. In return Beth told Graham that she had been having a private training session when the news had hit. This was essentially the truth but Graham obviously did not believe her. He could see that there was something between his wife and this working class yob who had infiltrated his way into their safe domain. Further investigation had led him to the shared bunks. He had not said much but it was obvious that he was very angry about it. Andy tried to approach him about the subject, despite Beth's warning. He had always thought that her husband had left her, rather than the other way around. It was something of a shock to find out that she had divorced her husband because of his violent tendencies and the fact that she had spent the last three Christmases in the intensive care unit in a private hospital.

Andy's attempt at bringing the situation into the open left him with a cracked lip and plenty of abuse. He could have fought back but in such tight quarters with nowhere else to go, it seemed that backing down and staying out of the guy's way was the best thing to do. The next day brought more unpleasantness, Graham was snappy with everyone, he had also taken stock of the food and called everyone together to announce that only three people could remain in the bunker.

"But there are four of us," Beth had said clenching her hands together in a nervous way.

"Yes, I can see that. There's also our daughter, or have you forgotten her?" Graham tossed over at his ex wife.

"But she's safe," Beth said," her eyes grew wide, her lips trembled. "She's miles away in school."

"Nowhere is safe Beth," her husband spat out. "The whole country is affected. Did you think it was just a local phenomenon?"

"I, didn't think," Beth started

"You never did, that was one of your problems," Graham carried on puffing himself up.

"Just hold your horses. Let's all stay calm shall we?" Andy knew he must make a stand, he was about to find himself on the street.

"Don't start with me or you will find yourself on the floor again," Graham said his eyes averted.

"I don't think you want to try that again. I may not play so nice next time," Andy stood up and leaned close to Graham's ear. "Next time you'll be the one on the floor and you won't get up so quick."

Graham pushed his chair back and stood up, the two men faced each other and something in Andy's eyes told Graham that it would be best to let it go.

"What I am saying is that our nineteen year old daughter is coming here and will need our support. Now I paid for this shelter, whatever her mother says, and I want my daughter in here with us."

"You should have left her where she was." Beth blurted out in a flood of tears. "We are in the heart of it here. You saw things up there, how will Safroni get to us?"

A sudden noise on the intercom took their attention, they all crowded around the video system. There was movement above, three or four shapes moving around by the cameras then they saw disjointed animals that had once been human crawling around on all fours, sniffing at the cameras, clawing at the hatch. They had a scaly look to them, their noses had vanished, their hands had become reptilian claws, they were like giant lizards with a tuft of human hair on their heads and a lost look in their eyes.

"They can't get in," Graham was almost talking to himself. "We'll just stay put until the police get control out there.

 Andy glanced at Cleo, she had a hurt look on her face which was directed at Graham. He suddenly had the idea that Graham had known Cleo before, known her intimately.

"What are you saying then?" Andy heard himself asking as the creatures continued to mill around the cameras. "Are you saying that you want me and Cleo to leave when your daughter arrives?"

"No, I'm not saying that," Graham avoided Andy's gaze.

"I didn't think you were," Andy said with an ugly look in Cleo's direction. "What do you mean then?" Beth had caught the look, though it had not been what Andy intended.

"Look it's quite clear that you're shacked up with this guy," her husband spoke calmly with authority as if his suggestion was completely normal.

"You will leave with him and that will leave enough food for the young girls and myself."

"Why don't you leave with me and leave the three ladies here together," Andy asked.

"Safroni is my daughter, I need to protect her. I can't leave her mother to do that."

"What about me," Beth asked "Don't I get any consideration, I want to be with Safroni too. I am her mother"

"We just don't have enough provisions," Graham had closed the matter, or so he thought.

"This girl can go, Andy will take her and watch out for her. This is my house now, my shelter, I won't let you take everything away from me. I'll kill you first," Beth kept her distance from Graham as she spoke, there was a desperation in her voice, an emptiness to her threat.

"Graham, you said I'd be safe here. You said we'd have it to ourselves just the two of us. I don't understand," Cleo started to cry, she held out her arms to Graham but he pushed them aside.

"Just someone you saved on the way," Beth said bitterly and turned away.

The monsters continued to mill around for a couple of hours, no-one was talking much. Andy had tried to comfort Beth though he did not know what to say. Eventually Beth stopped crying and went over to the corner where Graham and Cleo had taken up residence. Andy watched as Cleo moved away. Beth had sunk to her knees, her hands clasped Grahams hands imploring him for something, trying to appeal to his better side, if he had one. Then, after a few moments, they suddenly hugged, it took both Cleo and Andy by surprise. For the next hour, Graham and Beth sat next to each other talking and occasionally laughing as if they were in total agreement with each other.

After that Beth went back to Andy, Cleo hastily returned to Graham's side but he was cool with her, not wanting to show affection.

"So what's up?" Andy asked trying to sound as nonchalant as possible.

"We have agreed that Safroni will stay here with her father," she paused, not for effect but because she knew what she was about to say would be the end of her. "I'm going to stay too. We are going to be a family again. I'm sorry I can't help you stay out of this mess but perhaps by the time Safroni gets here with Martin, our bodyguard, everything will be better, those things will have moved on."

"Do I look like Bruce Willis to you?" Andy asked with a raw edge to his voice.

"Bruce… no I wouldn't say there was much resemblance, a little maybe," Beth was obviously caught off guard by the question.

"I thought maybe I looked like him so you thought I was some sort of hero about to do battle single-handedly." Andy stood up and backed away from her, she looked surprised, it aggravated him.

"You don't decide who lives and dies. Your husband waltzes in who nearly killed you before and all of a sudden you're eating out of his hand," Andy felt his anger rising.

"No it is for my daughter. I need to be with her."

"To protect her from him?" Andy said much more loudly than he intended to. Graham was making his way over.

"Please, I like you Andy, don't make this harder than it is. You have more chance out there. I think there is just the one thing out there now." A lizard type creature was banging on one of the cameras. It's lips drawn back, the eyes bright and quizzical.

Andy glanced towards the video screens. "I don't think any of us stand much chance out there. More to the point I'm not the one who'll be leaving. What did he say to you?"

"We talked about Safroni, how good she is, how special. She is the reason I stuck it with Graham as long as I did. There is a holiness about her," Beth's lip trembled.

"A what!" Andy cried.

"Shh, he never touched me when she was around. There was a peacefulness about her. A beautiful child, never ill, happy all the time, caring for all other creatures"

"Hey, I'm a vegetarian, it doesn't make me Ghandi."

"She's not a vegetarian," Graham's voice made him jump.

"So much for the animal loving part," Andy said as he prepared to square off with Graham.

"She's special. Calming, Loving. A wonderful child," Beth's voice trailed away.

"Yes and when Martin finds an opportune time he'll bring her to us," Graham put his arm on Beth's shoulder.

"And who the hell is Martin?" Andy asked weighing up his chances of beating Graham in a fight.

"He works for me. Takes care of things, I'll probably have him take care of you when he gets here."

"And where does he fit into your trio?" Andy glanced at Beth but he already knew the answer. Martin was going to get thrown to the wolves as well.

"We'll see," Graham said quietly.

Their attention was caught by Cleo's scream. She pointed to the video displays.

A man with blood streaming down his face was banging on the hatch. He was kicking at the lizard creature and had a shot gun which he kept firing and reloading.

"Martin!" Beth's voice was small and distant.

217

"Get the hatch open," Graham cried. "Get them in. We'll figure who goes out later."

Beth ran to the hatch and tapped the number in. Nothing happened. She tapped it in again. Nothing happened.

"Get it open," Graham cried. "Safroni!"

They could see Safroni's face from under Martin's coat, terrified and calling for her mother. Andy watched as she screamed and as claws ripped into Martin's arm, there was still more than one creature out there.

Graham dug his fingers into Beth's shoulders and told her to remember the number, to get their daughter in.

Andy rushed over and started to tap the number in he had reprogrammed the day before.

"What the hell are you doing," Graham said through gritted teeth.

"I changed it," Andy called back over his shoulder. He punched in the eight number figure.

"You changed it," Beth said hitting him with her fist on his cheek. He shrugged off the brief flare of pain and punched in the eight figure number again. Nothing happened.

Graham pushed Beth aside, "Why doesn't it open? What have you done."

"I changed it to this number. I know it's right," Andy put the numbers in again, slowly and carefully. Still no response. "I don't understand."

"You can't just reprogram it without the key sequence, all you've done is make it reset to its original state. Now I have to get the manual," Graham rushed off to one of the large cupboards and pulled everything out. At the bottom was a secret panel where the manual was kept. He pried at the panel till his nails bled glancing at the screens every few moments, terrified that he would be too late. Then he had the manual and rushed back to the hatch panel.

Beth's eyes were still glued to the screen. Martin was running out of energy, he had two shot guns. He would fire one and then grab the other which Safroni would have reloaded. They looked like the finale of a silent action film as the bodies of the lizard people fell around them. Only two lizards remaining but they were standing their ground, changing their eyes bulging their backs becoming more upright. They sat down on their haunches as the changes continued.

Martin changed the position of the shotgun and held it as if it were a club, he showed Safroni how to do the same with the other one. They were out of bullets.

Graham started punching numbers into the dial as he reset the lock. He could hardly see as the tears started to stream down his face.

"Hurry," Beth cried, her body quivering with short gasps of fear and desperation.

Graham stopped and sank to the ground.

"Get up, get up and reset it!" Beth kicked at him on the floor. "Quick before those things start moving again.

Martin was mouthing at the video cameras, he didn't know that they couldn't hear him. "Why?" he kept repeating. The creatures were starting to move again, they now stood on two legs with humanoid arms but their eyes were dark, unseeing. Martin's face lost all hope, he whispered something to Safroni and she started crying again. He lifted the butt of the shotgun, he was going to kill her, to save her from being torn apart by these things or whatever else they might do.

Beth screamed and pawed at the video screens. Her voice was too cracked for any audible words to come out. Andy grabbed Graham and shook him hard.

Graham just held up the manual with pages of numbers to be tapped in and pointed to the words underneath the sequence, "It will take approximately twenty minutes to set your new code."

Andy flicked through the pages, there had to be something.

Martin had lowered the shotgun butt and Beth almost fainted with relief but Andy knew that he had just been lining the weapon up, the next time he raised it, it would come down hard on Safroni's skull and crush the life from her. He was just waiting for the eyes to clear and monsters to resume their attack, waiting in the futile hope that the hatch would open.

He reached the back of the manual and there it was in bold print. "In an emergency the hatch may be opened by tapping in 0000. This may only be done from inside the hatch."

The eyes were clearing on the creatures, they pulled themselves up to full height. Martin closed his eyes, he was praying, his hand gripped the butt and raised it quickly into the air and then made a swift movement down.

The hatch had opened, Martin had veered his deathly course at the last moment, he pushed Safroni down the hatch and tumbled in after her pulling it shut as he did so.

They lay in a heap at the bottom of the ladder. Beth and Graham had grabbed Safroni and were hugging her on either side.

Andy started punching the numbers in to reset the lock. He hoped he would have twenty minutes before blame was passed around as most of it would land on him. Cleo was sitting quietly on her bunk. She had sat there for most of the drama, her eyes looked blank as though fear had already won her soul.

Graham was suddenly pulled to his feet and hit with a velocity that sent him sprawling across the floor. Martin stood over him dripping blood from his open wounds on arms and face. A long gash along his cheek still bled uncontrollably. Andy momentarily lost his place in the reset. Up close he could see that Martin was a big man with obvious survival skills, one not to be messed with. There would be no keeping the code from him if he wanted it. Andy dropped the manual, he was sure that he was about to be beaten up or killed.

"What the hell, Graham?" Martin could hardly get the words out he was filled with rage. He looked at the video screens, the two remaining creatures still wandered around. "Why didn't you let us in?"

Graham rolled over and looked up at him with his remaining eye, the other had closed as the swelling had engulfed it. "I tried, this idiot changed the code and didn't tell anyone."

Martin's gaze turned to Andy.

"Hey, I tried to get it open, it didn't work, but I did get you eventually – I was the one who got the hatch open."

Martin's rage seemed to be subsiding, he didn't know who this fool was, but he could see that the man was muscular and could probably put up a fight and he'd had enough of that for now.

"We mustn't fight now," the voice had a pure quality to it, a soothing reassuring ring about it.

All eyes turned towards Safroni.

"We must all work together, be friends," She glanced at Martin and then Andy, "we will survive."

"She has the voice of an angel," Andy heard himself say and then he realized that the cuts on Martin were bites and he wondered if there would be any infection.

Martin went to a cot in the corner and lay down. Apparently he had not slept for two days in his determination to get Safroni to her father. Andy knew that it would only be a matter of time until the rations were counted and some of the people expelled from the safety of the bunker. Cleo and he were definitely getting kicked out, he thought probably Beth too. That would depend on

Safroni and how much control she had over her father and her bodyguard and whether she really was as pure as she seemed.

Chapter 19

Little more was said for a few hours. Darkness had fallen and there was no sign of the creatures. Martin lay on one of the cots face down. His big body heaved and his breathing seemed laboured. Beth watched him with some apprehension, she had noticed the blood on him, the bites. Beth and Martin were sitting quietly at the table with their daughter, they just held hands and looked at each other.

Cleo had disappeared into the darker reaches of the bunker, Andy presumed she was taking a nap and feeling pretty sorry for herself. She had probably realized that she was not going to be allowed to stay and eat Safroni's precious rations.

Andy went to the table and sat down at the opposite end to the happy united family.

"Look, we all need to stick together to get through this." Andy said.

Both Beth and Graham looked at him with steely expressions, no allies there.

"Hello, my name is Safroni," the girl said.

Andy was taken back, there was something unusual about her, something calming. Hard to believe that she was related to these two.

"I'm Andy," he said.

"You don't need to know who he is," Graham put in, "he isn't staying."

"Oh but he can't go out there," Safroni said. " Not yet, it is too horrible. There are horrible things out there. They were at my school. They killed people at my school. People I knew. My friends and teachers. If Martin hadn't shown up when he did, they might have killed me."

"Might?" Andy said.

"Yes, he rescued me from them. They had locked me in a cupboard with Julia. But we could still hear them killing people outside."

"Why didn't they kill you?" Andy asked, a prickle went down his spine.

"I don't know." Safroni looked down and suddenly the innocence around her seemed to be hiding something else.

"How old are you'? Andy asked, though he could sense that Graham was getting tired of hearing him speak.

"Nineteen," Beth answered.

"Julia was my best friend," Safroni continued. "I don't even know what happened to her. Martin broke us out and then carried me off, just slung me over his shoulder." She laughed nervously. "I could see Julia was trying to follow us but she couldn't keep up and then we were in the car and driving away." She broke off and put her head in her hands.

"It wasn't your fault, he didn't save your friend," Andy said gently.

"I told Martin to get Saf out, not to worry about anyone else." Graham said.

Martin began to stir on the bunk. He sat up, his wounds seemed less, his eyes bright.

Andy didn't like the way Martin was moving, it seemed unnatural. Maybe he would be better off out of the bunker. He went over to the hatch and peered out into the darkness.

"I'd like to take a weapon with me," Andy said. "If I'm going out there, I'd like to take a weapon for protection." He already had his hand on the shot gun which everyone else seemed to have forgotten.

"We might need it," Graham said.

"Sure you might," Andy glanced at Martin "Even so, its going with me."

"Beth, if you want to come with me," Andy knew she would say no but he had to ask her.

Martin stood up, he seemed taller and his eyes were clicking everywhere.

"I don't feel well," Martin said and sat down again.

Andy locked eyes with graham and they both knew that Martin was infected. Andy started to open the hatch.

"Wait," Graham called , "help me get Martin out and I'll let you stay.

Andy shook his head. "Sorry, he looks a bit too strong and I don't want to get that close to him."

"Well then shoot him," Graham said. "Or give me the gun and I'll do it, think about the women."

Andy didn't know anything about guns except he was fairly sure that this one was empty. " "Its little more than a club," he said " you could see it was empty in the fight or Martin would have been using it."

Graham went over to one of the shelves and fished at the back. He walked over to Andy with a box of shotgun bullets.

"Take care of Martin before you go and I will let you take the gun," He held out the box of bullets.

Andy looked over at the girls, Cleo had reappeared, her eyes red from crying. She had a canvass bag slung over her shoulder he noticed. She moved over to his side.

"I'll come with you," she said in a whisper. "I realize that there is no place for me here," she said to Graham.

"I am sorry Cleo. However, I need to see what you have in the bag. We can't afford to let our food go. You can get more out there." Graham reached for the bag but Cleo jumped away and stood behind Andy.

Graham's eyes hardened. "Okay, take care of Martin first and you can go."

Andy reached for the hatch and put his new code in. He had written it down and left it on the floor so that the others could get it after. Andy flipped the hatch open and peered out half expecting to get his head ripped off. It seemed quite out there. Just a few dead monster bodies.

A scream from Beth made him stop and jump back inside. Martin was moving now, his head bent on one side, his body contorted, he drooled and his teeth were becoming pointed. Andy threw the gun to Graham.

"I don't know how to use it," Andy shouted

Graham quickly flipped open the gun and loaded it but before he could close it again, Martin's hand closed round his throat and threw him against the wall. His spine shattered on impact.

Beth was screaming hysterically, Cleo had already climbed out of the hatch.

Martin reached Beth and stood for a second mesmerized by Martin and the ongoing transformation. Martin seemed to be weigh Beth up, then he lashed out a clawed hand and sent Beth sprawling to the floor, then he leapt onto her and ripped into her head.

Andy grabbed Safroni's hand and dragged her up the hatch. Cleo stood transfixed at the top, not knowing which way to run. Andy led them around the front of the house to the drive and jumped into the car. The doors were open and the keys were still in the ignition. They could hear Martin following them up from the bunker. Cleo fell before the car a few feet from the car and Safroni ran back to help her. Creatures from nowhere seemed to be around them. Andy watched helplessly, he could have possibly reached them and knocked the creatures away.

Andy started the car and drove off, he didn't care which way, he just wanted to get away from the Martin creature who had appeared from the back and had ran towards the car.

Andy looked back in the rear view mirror. He could see Safroni standing over Cleo, her hands outstretched to the creatures to keep them at bay. Then they seemed to bow their heads before her. He slammed his breaks on and tried to get a better look at what was happening but she was obscured by many creatures now.

Andy put his foot down and drove away.

Chapter 20

Andy stood glued to his tracks. The first car that had stopped seemed to have normal people in it. But then there was something odd about one of the men that had got out. The other car had a friendly female driver, and yet she had smiled and waved as if all was right with the world. Now one of the men was walking towards him, but tentatively and was calling something he couldn't quite hear, then he did.

"It's not human! Come towards me." The man was calling and he was getting closer. Time to make a choice. Andy stood transfixed looking at the smiling woman, she was still waving, but now he could make out that one of her fingers was missing. He started to move towards Alex, then picked up some speed, practically running. The thing behind him slid back into its car, the expression on its face still had the smile plastered across it, rigour mortis had set in.

Alex had jumped back in the car, the back door remained open for Andy, he hesitated for a moment then jumped in. Alex sped off, he wanted to pick up some speed before the new guy took a good look at Frank.

"Thanks for stopping. Do you know what's going on?" Andy asked.

"My name is Samantha, this is Caroline, next to you, Alex driving. We escaped from London but that car seems to be following us. How did you survive?" Samantha sounded friendly but there was a nervousness to her voice and she had omitted to introduce the man on the other side of the child.

Andy glanced over to the stranger, his head was bowed, his hands in his pockets. He had been told to stay like that by Alex until he could be "explained."

"I was in a fallout shelter, too many people turned up and I had to leave. Don't think I would have survived out here alone." Andy glanced away, he found it difficult to maintain eye contact.

"We've all had a rough time," Samantha murmured.

"Can I say hello now?" Frank asked.

Andy looked across Caroline, she looked worried, the man on the other side put his head down again.

"Hey kid, my name is Andy Mermen."

"Hello," Caroline said and put her hand on Frank's arm. "This is my friend Frank. He's a bit different to us but he's perfectly okay."

Frank lifted his head briefly and nodded , "hello."

"What the hell….." Andy pushed himself against the door in an effort to get further from Frank.

Alex watched uneasily in the rear view mirror. "Just take it easy okay. He isn't one of them, just looks like one."

Andy had thought of leaping from the car but the other one was still following them at a distance and what other chance would he have. The monster lifted its head and smiled at him. The teeth were long, sharp and the eyes bloodshot, the skin sallow and pale. "I am Frank," it said. "I am a goodie."

"Yeah?" Andy asked, he looked into the rear view mirror and saw Alex watching him. "I bet you are," he answered. Frank held his taloned hand out to which Andy shrieked inwardly but shook the tip anyway. "

Pleased to meet you," Frank continued.

"Yeah, me too," Andy said quickly glancing round to see if the others looked normal.

"We didn't think we would come across anyone alive now, not infected." Alex watched Andy in the rear view mirror.

"Oh, I was in a bunker for a while but then it got too crowded, some of us had to leave."

"A bunker!" Sam said with more excitement than she meant to. "Army?"

"No, a do it yourself under the garden type, I'm afraid," Andy replied lightly. Frank was peering at him with some intensity.

"How many of you were there? Should we go and let them know we are alive?" Samantha asked looking at Alex.

"Not much point," Andy broke in, "They wouldn't let you in, they were throwing people out, as I said before."

"Yes, as you said before," Alex glanced in the mirror to see if the car was still following them, it appeared to have stopped. "Maybe it wasn't really following us," he thought but he knew better, the real question was why it wasn't any longer.

"So, where are we headed?" Andy put on his friendliest, happy go lucky voice.

"Stansted to get a helicopter, if we're lucky," Alex placed his hand on Samantha's and squeezed it, she was looking pensive. She smiled and put her hand on his. Andy watched from the back and couldn't stop the scowl from crossing his face. Alex caught it in the mirror.

"Maybe we should go back and see these friends of yours after all," Alex said "After all, we should at least let them know what the situation is out here and they can't be that far back."

"There's no point, you would just be wasting your time. Besides, it looked like it was being over-run when I drove away, they are probably all dead." Andy looked down.

Alex stopped the car and turned to face Andy. "Switch places with Caroline, Frank."

"Oh okay." With a movement so swift that everyone in the car was surprised, Frank whisked Caroline over the top of him and was sitting next to Andy in a second. Frank allowed to let his teeth look sharper and more menacing as he felt that this is what Alex wanted.

"What's the deal?," Andy asked.

"We were so eager to pick you up, not having seen anyone else that looked normal that we forgot to see if you were dangerous," Alex said. He didn't like to stop where they were for long just in case something showed up but he didn't want to risk his group with an unknown factor like Andy.

"They're not friendly at the fallout shelter," Andy pleaded.

"I thought you said they were probably dead," said Samantha.

"Look whatever happened you can tell us, we won't judge you, these are difficult times." Alex lied.

"Okay, I was pushed out as a decoy, they expected the monsters to go for me as they made a run for it. But for some reason," Andy faltered slightly " they weren't interested in me, I had a chance to get to a car and locked myself in. When I looked back they were crowding into the bunker. No-one else got out. I should have gone back to help them. There was a child, I should have helped her." Andy put his head in his hands. He sounded sincere, looked sincere and yet something wasn't sincere about his story. Alex couldn't probe any further without upsetting the girls and whatever had happened, he didn't think the man seemed violent and if he was he didn't want to force his hand.

Frank started tutting. "Oh dear, tut, tut, oh dear, tut tut. What a load of crap." Frank said and picked his nose with a claw.

So much for not forcing his hand Alex thought.

Andy looked up. "I can't make you believe me, but why would I lie?
"

"It's all right." Alex said as he drove the car off "pay no attention to him. He says that to everyone."

"Do I? Tut tut." Frank said and started humming.

"I'm just glad you picked me up. I won't let you down I promise." Andy was pleading with his eyes in the rear view mirror and yet there was something else behind them, something hard.

They arrived at Stansted, it appeared deserted and located a Lear jet in one of the hangers.

"Where are we heading?" Andy asked.

"America. Europe has been as badly hit as Britain," Alex replied.

"How do you know?" Andy glanced at Frank.

"Lets just say I get insider information." Alex replied. "Go with Frank to the little office at the back and look for keys to get us into the jet."

"You can fly one of those things?" Andy asked with unmasked respect.

"I can fly that one, " Alex responded. "It's Mine."

Frank was singing "Airport" again and hopping on one leg towards the booth. Andy followed silently, wondering how much better he was with these people.

"Do you think we should get some supplies before we fly off," Samantha asked.

"We'll check what's on board first and see if the radio is working. Plus we should see if there is anyone around. We could get a few people away in this thing and I can't help but feel there are more survivors hiding somewhere." Alex looked towards the terminal.

"Do you think Andy's friends survived? Are you thinking of going back to look?"

"No, I don't think he knows anyone that made it but I can't help but feel that there is someone here. I want you and Caroline to get in the plane. I will check out the terminal with Frank and Andy."

"No, you're not leaving us alone," Samantha grabbed his arm "and you're not leaving Frank behind."

Alex let his guard drop and his eyes betrayed him. He had every intention of leaving Frank behind. Now she was angry with him again. He really wanted them to get some time together away from the little psycho party and Caroline, just a few short minutes to tell her how he felt for so long now.

"Frank stays with us," Samantha said as she flounced off to help Frank and Andy look for the keys to the plane.

"Great! Send Andy over here" Alex called after her. "Frank will be easy to explain in Washington. They'll probably shoot him on sight," he added softly. Getting on board the jet with Frank and Andy was going to be like travelling with two time bombs on board for six hours or so.

Andy came trotting over. "That...guy is completely mad."

"You must mean Frank."

"Whatever you call it. He grabbed the keys and wouldn't let me near them, kept sticking up two of his talons at me."

"Alex said as he grabbed a pistol from the boot of the car.

Alex grabbed the shotgun from the boot.

"And we are going where?" Andy asked

"Into the terminal, make sure we have enough supplies and to see if there are any survivors here. Do you know how to handle a gun?"

Andy sighed, "I "m not good with guns."

Alex gave him a hand gun, "just point and shoot.

"Suddenly you trust me with a gun? I was getting the impression that you didn't believe anything I said?"

Alex smiled "Sure I trust you, besides I don't die easily."

The two of them started walking to the terminal. They couldn't see anyone around but Alex could feel something, a survivor somewhere but now he could also feel them. The terminal wasn't going to be empty.

"Whatever we find in there, just follow my lead," Alex said.

"No problem" Andy said trying to get the safety off his handgun.

The lights were still running, music was playing in the brightly lit hallway.

"Do we have any idea where we are going?" Andy asked.

"To the duty free," Alex said.

They made their way slowly, half expecting things to leap out at them. If there were hordes of zombies here they would have seen them by now. They had almost reached duty fee. They went in and Alex sensed what he was looking for was hiding in the back room. He moved behind the till area and put his hand on the door.

"How do you know it isn't full of creatures?" Andy asked.

"I just do," Alex said slightly agitated suddenly by Andy's presence. "Why don't you go and find some food to take with us. Sandwiches, whatever you can find."

"Yeah okay, there isn't exactly a supermarket here. I'll hit Smiths though, at least get some chocolate and that to keep us going." Andy paused. " You gonna be all right on your own?"

Alex smiled and turned back to him, "Sure, thanks. I'll meet you back here in twenty minutes."

"Okay," Andy seemed to want to say more but he just shrugged and headed off to the bright lights of Smiths.

Alex turned his attention back to the door. There was someone behind it, he was sure, but something wasn't right. He turned the handle, a strange smell filtered out. He flicked the switch on and the room was illuminated. The room was empty but a large cupboard opposite him was slightly ajar and he could just hear heavy breathing.

"It's okay, we won't hurt you. We've come to rescue you." He advanced slowly towards the cupboard and could pick up the feelings of the creature in the cupboard. It was very scared and yet it trusted his voice, it was coming out.

Alex stepped back as a large dog walked towards him from the cupboard. It's head was massive, a black muzzle and black ears with deep red fur about the height of a Great Dane with the weight of a mastiff.

"Hello girl, how long have you been in there. You must be pretty hungry."

The dog put her head down so that he could pet her.

Andy came up behind him, "If that's the only survivor, we should get back to the jet," Andy wriggled on his feet. He felt uncomfortable around the huge dog.

"She's a survivor all right, but there are other things here."

The dog stood and wagged her tail then walked forward, she waited.

"I think she wants us to follow her," Alex said.

"Yeah? You do that then, I'm heading on back." Andy started to walk towards the hanger. Suddenly a zombie was walking towards him. it stopped and smiled.

Alex looked into its eyes.

Andy was shaking. All the monsters he had seen, he could tell himself were mutations, a virus that was affecting people. But this thing in front was a dead body. A walking dead body, the decay was all over it. When alive she had probably been a beautiful girl but now her hair had partly fallen out and her hand had a finger missing.

"She's the thing from the road," Andy said edging back towards Alex and the dog which Alex was now resting his hand on. The dog growled.

"She's more than that," Alex said.

"Hello Alex, I caught you. You and your friends. I just want to talk with you." She walked forward, her left leg dragged behind, her slowing her movement.

"I'm not waiting to see what she wants," Andy ran off towards the jet.

"What do you want?" Alex said.

"You," she said as she lifted her hand towards him.

Alex dropped the shotgun and felt something grip his chest and force him to the ground as she edged nearer to him. He body felt as though it were being pulled in all directions at once. The next moment she was on the floor, the pain was gone and the dog was dragging her away by the shoulder.

"Need help?" Frank was at his side. Alex grimaced, that was the last thing he wanted from Frank but his legs felt weak, his head buzzing. he put his arm around Franks shoulder and frank helped him to his feet. Alex indicated the shotgun lying on the ground to Frank, but he just smiled and left it. He pulled Alex quickly along until they reached the jet. The further they got away from the zombie, the better Alex felt. By the time they reached the jet he could run on his own.

Caroline and Samantha were nowhere to be found.

"Where are they?" Alex said to Frank. "Were they here when you left?"

"No, they had already taken them, would have taken me to, if it weren't for the fact I ran away."

"You ran away. Why would you do that? Who took them?" Alex asked.

"Creatures, like me, not like me, like you, not like you. I've refuelled the jet while you were gone. You can get to America from here. Just you though."

"I'm not going without Samantha or Caroline," Alex said.

"Hmmm." Frank sat down on the ground and put his head in his hands.

"Are you coming to look for them?
" Alex asked, not bothering to hide his contempt.

"It might see you again, it might kill you next time." Frank said melodically.

"It cant kill me" Alex said.

"It can," Frank said under his breath.

"What happened to the other guy, Andy, or whatever his name was? did you leave him behind to get killed by that thing?"

"Yes," Frank said. "He probably got killed, or he ran away. I suspect he ran. What do you think?"

Alex sat down next to Frank. "Why would you let them take Caroline and Samantha? I thought you would die for them?"

"I would", Frank "But, these things had to take them to keep them safe. To take them to where they need to be - where you can't be. I ran to save you, I knew you needed it. Now i will go and join them, but you can't come".

240

Alex grabbed Frank by the throat and forced him onto the ground. Frank lay there not moving. His eyes blank,"

"I don't understand, where are they?" Alex pleaded.

Alex was aware of someone near them and stood up. Frank sat up and smiled as if nothing had happened. Andy was out of breath, he moved over to them quickly.

"Did you forget someone" he shouted at Frank.

"You seem okay" Frank replied, his long fingernail trailed across his cheek.

"No thanks to you" Andy spat back. "You just left me, it could have killed me".

"Why didn't it?" Asked Alex.

"The dog, it stopped it, chewed it up and then the dog just ran off".

"So you're fine", Frank said and hopped to his feet. "You should go with Alex, he is going to New York".

Alex smiled coldly "Not without Samantha and you are going to tell me which way they went, in fact, you are going to tell me where they are, because I don't think you would have let them go unless you knew where they were being taken".

Frank looked at the jet and then back to Alex. He made a snorting noise towards Andy. he turned away and then suddenly leapt through the air grabbing Andy by the throat and pinning him to the ground.

Alex was about to pull him off when Frank shot him a look and tightened his grip around Andy's throat.

'Frank? Why font you let him go?' Alex asked.

Frank released Andy enough for him to speak.

'Tell us what happened at the bunker', he whispered with his long tongue into Andy's ear.

'I killed them', Andy spluttered.

'All of them?' Frank pushed.

'Yes, no. All except her, except', Andy stopped as Frank let go and stood away.

'There was a survivor' Frank said half in a dream.'You couldn't kill her. She is ours'.

Frank ran from the bunker on all fours so fast that he was gone, before Alex had time to stop him. Alex ran after him but there was no trace. He sank to the ground, he felt empty, a gnawing feeling in his stomach, he had lost her.

Alex returned to the jet, Andy was leaning against it coughing and holding his throat.

'You can tell me what happened on the way to New York', Alex said without feeling.

'What you just gonna leave? I thought you were in love with that woman and pretty fond of the girl too. Are you going to leave them behind?'

Alex stopped next to Andy and looked at him with cold, unseeing eyes. 'They aren't here anymore. I would sense them. Frank would not let anything happen to them. ' A movement behind caused him to look round.

The big dog was back. it looked at him with sad eyes. 'You must go', it said 'it will be overrun here. they are coming'

'Samamtha? ' Alex asked

'Safe, as long as you leave. if you die. She dies', the dog replied.

Alex shrugged, 'I can't die'.

'Yes' the dogs words echoed in Alex's mind. 'I know it, and frank knew it to. The things that are here can kill you and ' suddenly the words screamed in Alex's head ' they are coming!'

The dog ran forward and jumped onto the jet.

A loud commotion could be heard on the tarmac, Alex went to the doors and looked out. There seemed to be hundred of dead people spreading out along the runway making their way towards him. These were not infected, these were dead, the ones that he realises, could kill him and wanted nothing but him.

He ran back to the jet and jumped aboard, Andy saw the things and jumped in behind him and closed the door.

They had already arrived in the hanger.

Alex started the aircraft.

'Aren't you supposed to do a load of checks' Andy asked.

'Shut up', Alex said and the jet started to roll forward.

Suddenly the dead were all over it. Banging on the roof, on the side panels. They were throwing themselves as hard as they could and as the broken bodies fell, more took their place.

Alex pushed the throttle forward and the jet ran over them, pushed them from the path. The dead held on to any part they could, even as it started to take off they still hung on, knowing that if they could not stop it, he would be gone and they may have to wait for the next chance to kill him which could be too late.

The dog whimpered as the jet took off. She was not keen on flying in such a backwards device and also she was supposed to remain here. But that would have meant certain death amongst so many dead things.

The jet was in the air now, they were safe at least from the decaying corpses on the ground.

Alex called Andy to take the co-pilot's chair. He wanted to know where he was at all times and know what he was doing. Something not right about him.

'Tell me what happened with the people in the bunker', Alex asked.

'Could take a while', Andy said.

'We have nine hours till we reach New York' Alex said.

The dog walked over to sit between them and showed her teeth to Andy with a low growl.

'I think she is saying that just tell the truth whatever that is because I don't fancy your chances with her if you don't Alex said.

Andy started to tell the story of the bunker to Alex. He reached the part where Martin became something else and killed Graham and Beth. Then he remembered it the way it had really been. He hadn't tried to help Safroni; He had barged out of the door and knocked Cleo aside. He had made it to the car and got in but then discovered that Cleo had the keys. He didn't know when she had got them but she stood there now, as the things started to surround her and shook them at him. She knew he would have to go back to her to get them and the tears in her eyes begged him to help her. He jumped out of the car and ran into the creatures knocking them into one another. Martin was just emerging from the hatch. Andy grabbed the hatch and swung it onto Martin's head, he saw him fall backwards. His head split, he looked dead so Andy jumped in with him. It now seemed safer to be in the bunker than outside. Cleo saw what he was doing and ran to get in to but he pushed her away and into the arms of a creature beside her which bit into her neck.

Safroni was kneeling a few feet away not looking at anything. Andy had no intention of helping her into the bunker either. He moved down the steps and was about to lock the hatch when a hand grabbed his leg. It was Martin, his brain hanging out from the spit head but it was still connected. His eyes yellow, spit running down the side of his mouth. Andy screamed and kicked his head backwards then pushed back through the hatch. He grabbed the keys where Cleo had dropped them and then grabbed Safroni. He used her as a shield in front of him. They seemed to be making a path for her, they didn't want to hurt her. 'She is one', they were chanting, those that had sufficient mental capacity to do so the others just drooled in unison.

He reached the car, it didn't have much gas but it would be enough to get away from here. They were advancing now, they did not want him to take their prize so he pushed her as hard as he could into them and they gathered around her. She screamed once and looked at him but he looked away, closed the car door and drove off. In the rear view mirror he could see her standing there amongst them but they were not hurting her. They were worshipping.

'When we land I want you to take the dog and go to an address I will give you. I need to keep this dog safe. This is your chance to do something right for once. Make up for past mid-deeds. do you understand me?' Alex asked

'Yes.', Andy said. he intended to dump both of them on arrival and get to as safe a place as possible.

'By the way', Alex continued, 'If you don't do as I say, I will hunt you down and kill you. Just go where I tell you and look after the dog. She is an important part of this. Okay?'

'Yes, I already agreed', Andy said. He decided he would do as he was told after all. The thought of this man tracking him down was more frightening that any monster he could think of.

'The army will be looking out for incoming aircraft but I know a place we can land quickly before they get to us. Set you on the right path. I will then go with them and see what they know'.

'That's just fine', Andy said and looked at the dog, which silently showed her teeth.

Chapter 21

A ship had arrived it had been full of British subjects alive and well proclaiming their escape from a dead country. There were several hundred on the boat. They weren't allowed to dock in New York but remained offshore. Daniel was taken with his new team of Deadlanders to investigate.

The QE2 sat calmly on the waters a little under a mile from the dock. There was little visible movement from the deck, the mob which had been cheering and making signs to low flying helicopters had vanished, only a small dog remained visible, sitting, waiting for the military to be airlifted aboard.

Daniel looked down from the helicopter, he had six men in his team, each armed to the teeth and wearing face masks to prevent contamination. He, on the other hand, wore no face mask and carried no weapon, his team eyed him nervously, feared and distrusted him.

"I'll go first then, shall I?" Daniel did not really expect a response.

"Fine." He attached himself to the winch and was hoisted down to the deck. The dog wagged its tail.

On closer inspection, the small dot of a dog was actually a rather large looking golden creature. He resembled a lion with a dog's black face. He was about the same height as a Great Dane but from the bulk of his body, Daniel would have estimated his weight at more than twelve stone.

The dog moved over to where Daniel had landed on the deck and stopped a couple of feet away.

"Good dog," Daniel tried to sound friendly, the helicopter noise above him was drowning out everything else. The dog lay down, wagging it's bushy tail.

Daniel beckoned for the other members of his team to join him. They did so one at a time, each keeping a wary eye on the dog. The helicopter flew back to port.

"Is it coming back for us?" Daniel asked

"You're in charge," Aldrich answered. "Don't you know what it's doing?"

Daniel shrugged. "Why don't you take care of the military aspects of this job?"

Aldrich smiled. "Okay, It will return for us on my command. We'll go through decontamination back at port head quarters."

So this is the way it is going to be Daniel thought and nodded. "You still obey my orders on the ship, right?"

"Yes, sir." Aldrich's smile disappeared.

Daniel remembered back to the selection of men for his team. They had all seemed to have their own agenda, which seemed to mainly entail killing him at some point. Although he was in charge because of his inside connection with the creatures, nobody really wanted him around. He snatched his thoughts back to their training together, that was not something he wanted to remember when their lives might depend on each other.

"Permission to shoot the dog?" Dorvel was asking, his weapon trained on the quizzical dog. It had stood up and was moving closer to Daniel.

"Permission denied," Daniel said. He put his hand down and the dog wagged its tail again.

"Are you expecting us to take it back with us on the helicopter sir?" Aldrich asked, his eyes resigned to the answer.

"We'll see." Daniel said as he fluffed up the giant dog's ears and it offered a huge paw. Daniel examined it, "webbed feet, must be a good swimmer."

A loud noise below them took everyone's attention. Something was happening.

"We'll take these doors first, move down onto the next deck. Anyone looks infected, shoot to kill." Aldrich looked at Daniel waiting for his response.

"We're not looking for a cure then?" Daniel stepped in front of Aldrich.

"My orders are specific. Not to let the USA become infected with this virus. Nothing gets off this ship alive that looks or even walks funny. Non negotiable."

Daniel was wondering why he was even there, but followed the others towards the door. They smashed it open, their weapons cocked, ready to take out whatever emerged, but nothing did.

Aldrich moved down the stairs first, Dorvel followed, Reeser, Widham, Fell and Bryson after. Daniel was about to follow when the dog took hold of his sleeve and pulled him back. It whimpered at him and pawed at the ground.

"It's all right boy, you stay here. There's a good dog" Daniel saw a piece of rope on deck and quickly tied it to the dogs collar. "Keep you out of harm's way and stray bullets, eh." The dog lay down and put his head on his paws.

Daniel hurried down the steps and found the others waiting for them. They glared with such malice that he nearly laughed.

"Did they issue you with a weapon for me?" He asked

"We were told you wouldn't need one," Aldrich responded.

Daniel shrugged, "Lead on then."

They made their way along a dimly lit passage the lights were wavering on and off. Two double doors were ahead of them which led to the main ballroom.

Aldrich stood on one side of the door and beckoned to Dorvel, he moved forward and pushed the door handle down.

The ballroom was well lit, the chandeliers glowing with pride. The men stood in the doorway frozen, their eyes peered into the vast room with its hundred or so tables surrounding the dance floor. Each table was fully occupied with humanoids, their heads turned sharply to the doors as they flew open.

"Sir?" Dorvel was saying, "should we open fire, we don't have enough bullets."

Daniel didn't really hear Dorvel's voice, his eyes were busy scanning the faces of the creatures before him. These were pale things, almost human, just looking and resting after a hearty dinner waiting for the dinner cabaret or dessert and something told Daniel that they could be it.

"Sir!" Dorvel's voice was louder, more insistent. He looked from Daniel to Caymen, neither seemed to be taking any notice of him. He pointed his gun at the nearest table. All the faces were looking directly at him, even the ones with their back to him, their heads had just swivelled on their necks to face him. All around the room many people had their heads on backwards looking at the soldiers, waiting for their dinner.

"Lower the gun," Daniel said quietly. This was something new, these were not contaminated in the way he had seen before, these were in civilized poses, apart from their heads. Their fingers looked normal, no talons, not yet. Their teeth were unseen hidden behind closed mouths and expressionless faces. But the eyes, there was something growing in the eyes, something Daniel understood. It was recognition.

Dorvel still pointed his gun at the first table, his hand shook and his finger itched on the trigger.

"We are going to back out of the room and close the doors," Aldrich said.

"Are we heading back already?" Daniel said. All the eyes in the room moved to him as he spoke. The soldiers saw it to.

Aldrich and the others were already backing out, Daniel took a step backwards towards the doors and a movement ran round the room. Everyone had started to stand. Daniel stopped and the creatures remained in place.

"Oh .." Aldrich said something under his breath and continued to back out of the room with the others. Daniel remained still.

The others were in the hall again and started to close the doors.

"Er, guys. You aren't leaving me here are you?" Daniel asked.

The sound of his voice made the hair stand up on the neck of every creature in the room, they all smiled. Jagged, pointed teeth.

"If you run for the doors, they'll be all over us," Aldrich said. "Just stay in there with them while we check the rest of the ship for survivors. We'll come back for you when we've finished."

"What?" Daniel raised his voice as the door swung closed. He could hear them tying something to the doors to secure them. The creatures had all stood when he'd spoken, and they looked towards him now with red eyes.

One from the nearest table took a few paces towards him and stopped only a foot away. Daniel froze. It raised an arm towards him, its long finger extended, but it dared not touch him. They all looked at him, wondering what he was, who he was and whether he was meat or friend. Did he bleed or was he indestructible, they wondered and grew hungrier .

Aldrich and the others were already back on the deck. The dog was nowhere to be seen.

"Where the hell did that dog go, man?" Fell said. "Those things down there, what are we going to do about them and Daniel Mason?"

"Leave him. There aren't going to be any survivors here. They were all in that room, all dead, or something like it." Aldrich checked his gun. "The dog probably went the other way. It must have gone down below again.
"

"Let's just get off this ship and blow it up," Fell said.

"We can't," Aldrich watched the helicopter circling nearby. We can't go back without Mason… unless he's dead. We'll wait ten minutes then go back and check on that room, if he's dead, then we can get out of here."

"And if he isn't?" Fell asked.

"I don't know. My orders were to get him on board, see how those things reacted to him and to not leave without him. I guess we could see how they reacted. We'll just wait a bit."

"Shouldn't we try going down the other way, see about survivors?"

"It doesn't matter," Aldrich said. "Any survivors are to be shot on sight anyway. They are assumed to be contaminated. We're going to blow the ship as soon as we get off it."

Aldrich waved his arms in the air and the helicopter returned. It lowered the two boxes.

"Explosives? Why the secrecy," Reeser asked.

"The big brass didn't think Daniel would go along with this. He wants answers, we just want them dead and some of the brass want him dead too."

"Five minutes more and we'll go back for him, whatever is left. But we'll go the other way, in case they have got out." The soldiers moved to the other side of the ship and went slowly down the stairs.

Daniel felt extremely uncomfortable with the creature so close to him. He took a step to the side and was alarmed to see all the inhabitants of the hall take a step towards him. He tried to hear their thoughts but there was nothing. Just a feeling of confusion and hunger emanating from their seemingly crippled bodies.

At the other end of the hall there were other doors, straight across the ballroom and through the middle of them. Behind him he knew the doors were tied in some way, besides they may also be booby-trapped. Everyone else might think that he was indestructible but he had his doubts.

The door at the other end of the ballroom was slightly ajar, suddenly it was knocked open and the large golden dog walked into the room. The creatures eyes flitted over to the dog and then back to Daniel.

The dog proceeded to walk towards Daniel across the long dance floor. A few of the creatures were interested by the movement and started to follow him. They dragged their feet and fell into line behind him, more joining as he passed each table. The creature nearest Daniel turned it's head towards the dog and moved into it's path between the dog and Daniel. Daniel looked back at the door behind him, he was sure that he had the strength to crash through it. He took a step back, eyes flicked to him but then back to the dog as it continued to walk towards him. He took a couple more steps. He could probably rush the door from here and be up on deck before they could chase him. Then he could swim, if necessary to the shore. He readied himself to go and glanced once more at the dog. It had stopped and its tail wagged slowly, nervously, it was blocked on all sides by the creatures. The ones behind were close enough to touch its tail. One of them reached out pulled a piece of moulting fur from the dog's tail and put it in its mouth. The dog looked back and then at Daniel.

The moment was upon him, now was the chance to get through the door away from the hundreds of humanoid creatures which filled the room. He looked back as taloned hands tried to take hold of the golden dog and then flipped himself over kicking the nearest creature into another, whisking his way down the room towards the dog which now stood transfixed in the middle of the room. Daniel hit out with every limb on his being as he catapulted his way past the creatures and picked the dog up as he went past, putting it round his neck as if it weighed no more than a kitten. The creatures flew in every direction. Their mood had changed, their eyes were black, they howled so loudly that Aldrich and his men heard it on deck as they started to make their way back to the ballroom.

One creature got close enough to stick a talon in Daniel's shoulder and rip down on his back before he spun round and kicked it twenty feet into the air. Then he had reached the far door and was racing up the stairs. He could hear them behind him, but they were slow and clumsy. On the top deck he saw the helicopter hovering nearby and waved at it. It flew over as the creatures started to spill onto the deck. There was no time to be picked up, he jumped into the sea and started to swim away from the boat. The dog swam at his side, it's powerful webbed feet pushed it effortlessly through the water.

The helicopter lowered a rope and Daniel tied it around his waist, it hoisted him out of the water. Daniel scooped the dog from the sea as he was winched up. A few feet from the rim of the helicopter the rope stopped, a man was shaking his head down at Daniel and indicating the dog. It appeared that they had no intention of letting it on the helicopter. With a few swift movements of his hand Daniel pulled himself up the rope and onto the craft. The soldier had pulled a revolver but Daniel kicked it from his hand as he dropped the dog lightly into the vehicle.

There was too much noise for conversation so the soldier stood glaring at Daniel, his eyes moving warily to the dog even now, which sat placidly wagging its tail.

Back on the dock they were surrounded as soon as they landed. The pilot and soldier hopped out and joined the fifteen or so weapons that were pointed in Daniel's direction. Colonel Aintree stepped forward.

"We can't allow any contamination. That dog must be destroyed, you must see the reasoning behind it. We're killing people rather than risk infection, why should we make allowances for a dog?" He was using his reasonable voice but Daniel knew that behind that was the steely determination of a man who would destroy the whole helicopter if necessary.

"He's special,' Daniel said slowly. "I'm not that keen on dogs," he wondered if they could tell that he was lying the way he could when they did. "The creatures feared it, they stood aside and let him pass. They were going to kill me when he showed up and stopped them. He got me out of there. Look!" Daniel turned to show his blood soaked back where the creatures had wounded him. The cut was almost gone but the blood stained on the shirt was convincing.

Colonel Aintree thought for a few seconds, Daniel knew he was being weighed up. "Okay you and your new friend will have to be quarantined. Just in case they infected you with that talon cut." His eyes moved to the dog, it looked back at him as if it knew that its life depended on his decision. "After the quarantine we'll take the dog and run a few tests on him."

Daniel knew what that meant and he intended to deal with that when it arrived. "No problem," he said, he was good at lying. "Now what about those men we left behind?"

The colonel's face changed "we don't leave men behind." He looked over to the pilot who shook his head. The other soldier spoke, "There were screaming noises, only …. and the dog came out, we assumed the others were all dead."

"You assumed?" Aintree looked towards the ship and shook his head. "We need to go back and check. All this time spent on a dog could have cost the lives of my men." He gave Daniel a look that could have turned him to stone.

"Best if I go back alone," Daniel said. "Otherwise you'd be losing more men, plus there may still be survivors down there, we didn't get very far with the search."

"Maybe if you'd taken care of my men better," the Colonel retorted with his most icy stare.

"Maybe if they hadn't locked me in a room with a hundred zombies I would have felt differently towards them," Daniel glared back.

Aintree moved close to Daniel so that no one could hear. "At risk of infection let me just tell you this once. This is your team, these are your men, your dead landers, your chance to do something for your country or be dead, your choice. You lose all your men, you're finished."

"They weren't my choice of men," Daniel said as he jumped back into the helicopter. "Perhaps you haven't heard, I'm mankind's only chance for survival, you should take care of me."

"You're not the only one," the Colonel said as the helicopter started up, it lifted off the ground as Daniel whistled and the dog jumped back on board.

"Not a dog lover," Aintree scoffed, he could see Daniel rubbing the dog's ears and smiling. He turned to the nearest soldier to him, "If he doesn't bring every man back from that squad, shoot the dog next time you see it and say it was a miscommunication, Mr Mason needs to know who is in control."

Chapter 22

As Daniel was being taken back to the ship, Alex was being transported to the dock where Colonel Aintree waited. Colonel Aintree walked up to him and shook his hand as soon as he arrived. Alex sensed a falseness around his eyes, a veneer honed over the years to make people see what he wanted and for some reason he desperately seemed to want Alex's approval. As he released Alex's hand he started talking to him as if he had known him all his life. He was difficult to dislike and even more difficult to distrust but Alex knew he must question everything this man said.

"I had you brought here to help on a rescue mission. My men are trapped on that ship out there with, who knows how many plagueoids, Mr Mason has gone in but I think he put them in danger in the first place. He handpicked them and then abandoned them first chance he got. He's had contact with the plagueoids and they pass information on to him. He may have a contact on the ship or he may have been attempting to smuggle the virus out via a dog he has somehow picked up and lifted from the ship. I want you to destroy that on sight, he left it on the helicopter which I have recalled."

Alex looked at the Colonel cooly penetrating deep into his eyes, "Hasn't Daniel Mason been helping to fight the plagueoids?"

"In his own way." He paused for effect. "But people have died and to date he has saved no-one or given any impression that he wants to. The creatures believe him to be one of them, they call him Menarty."

Alex gave an involuntary movement with his expression and Aintree knew he had hit the right note. It appeared that the Colonel was out of the loop as far as Alex's real mission today.

"They take him over sometimes, they tell him to do things. Frankly, now that you're here, he's one risk we don't need," Aintree glowed inwardly, he knew that Cartier was aware of Menarty, could see it in his face and more could see that the name frightened him and that he wanted it destroyed.

The helicopter had returned from the ship and had just landed, the Colonel pointed over to it. "Better take care of the dog first."

The side door of the helicopter was open and Alex could see the dog sitting in the gloom, a large figure of unknown intent. Aintree had Alex loaded up with guns and ammunition.

"Better if I take the dog over the ocean and dispose of him there," Alex said his eyes averted.

"Whatever you think is best," Aintree's voice was harsh, he suddenly realized that he had not found an ally but maybe another enemy. "I'll send Sgt Raither with you, he'll lead you to the others." Alex nodded, they both knew where they stood.

The Colonel pointed towards where the dog peeked out. "There is more to my request on this animal than it seems. I like dogs as much as the next man, but this is no ordinary dog, you only have to look into its eyes."

Alex started to walk towards the helicopter, "Colonel, this is obviously some power struggle between you and Mason, he wants the dog alive and you don't." Alex dropped all the weapons and ammunition he had been given to the ground before hopping onto the helicopter, Raither jumped in behind him.

"This one's worse than the other one," the Colonel said under his breath, Alex heard him.

Meanwhile Daniel had been dropped to the ship, he had left the dog on the helicopter and believed it to be safe from the Colonel, he had told it to stay in the copter and the dog had given him a knowing glance, the dog seemed to understand full sentences. He had told the helicopter pilot that the dog's life was his responsibility and the man had seemed frightened enough to listen. Then he had made his way down to where he sensed the men were hiding, he hadn't expected the helicopter to return to the dock. A sudden pang of loss flittered through him and the hope that nobody would go against his wishes and hurt his new found friend.

Raither said nothing to Alex as the helicopter neared the QE2. He was a large dark man without a smile who had never questioned an order of any kind and lost no sleep over the atrocities which he had personally inflicted on others during his life. Alex sat next to the dog, he was a little wary of it because of the size and because he knew it would sense that he was different. It looked at him with golden eyes and he could see the faint wag of its tail in the gloom. He reached out and stroked under its muzzle. Raither made a noise as if clearing his throat but said nothing.

The helicopter hovered over the sea just before the ship. "This would be a good place to get rid of the dog."

"Maybe we should see what Mr Mason has to say about him first. He doesn't seem dangerous," Alex stroked a furry ear.'I've met a friend of yours," he whispered.

Without warning Raither pulled his revolver out and fired at the dog's head. Alex deflected it with his knuckle into the side of the copter, luckily not in a vital section. Raither's face was shocked into a grimace, the gun removed from his palm so quickly that he didn't have time to blink. "I guess they didn't really tell you anything about me," Alex said as he swiped Raither, knocking him out. The pilot was sweating, his whole body shook.

"Get as close to the deck as you can. I'll jump. Come back in thirty minutes. Oh and tell the Colonel I decided to take the dog with me. I'm handpicking people who work with me and this guy isn't one of them. However, I'll take the dog.

Alex jumped to the ship with the large dog under his arm. "Sorry about this boy. I know he got you off here once but a ship full of zombies is about as safe as it gets for you at the moment. Stay here"

Alex walked towards the wedged door but the dog trotted past him, it obviously intended to go with him. "Okay, you can find him for me," Alex said as the helicopter flew back to report to the Colonel. "I have a feeling we are going to need another way off this thing.

Daniel had already found the bodies of the missing men, there was no doubt that they weren't coming back from the dead, there wasn't enough left of them. He had begun a search of the cabins when the golden dog caught up with him, it put its paws on his shoulders and looked into his eyes, then it bumped noses with him lightly and looked behind it to where Alex stood watching.

There was almost an electrical current between the two men as they looked at one another, a connection that they didn't understand but were both amazed and terrified of.

"Alex Cartier," Daniel said , "or should I say Menarty?"

"I am no more Menarty than you, I hope," Alex advanced a little, the dog stood between them. "It doesn't have to be either one of us, they just think it is."

"You're referring to the aliens?" Daniel said

"If that's what they are," Alex replied. "I thought there was an undead thing going on here."

"They're alien and they're not alone. I believe there to be at least one other alien life-form currently on Earth."

Alex glanced away and thought of Caroline. He looked back at the dog, "Is that one?"

Daniel looked surprised, "He's just a big dog got caught up on the wrong ship, which I got him off," Daniel added with frustration and ruffled the dog's ears.

"He's safer here," Alex said as he moved closer to Daniel and held out his hand.

Daniel shook it and smiled, "It's nice to have an ally, finally."

Alex shook his head, "you do seem to have made some powerful enemies already. We may have trouble getting you off this ship, never mind anyone else we may find."

"That's just it, they told me that they weren't here to get survivors"

"Or maybe they just wanted us on this ship"

The thought was broken into by zombies at either end of the corridor. They stood transfixed for a moment looking at Alex, then their eyes widened, their mouths opened they screamed and charged.

Daniel jumped into the open cabin, Alex and the dog followed, they stood against the door as the creatures pounded on it for a few seconds. Then they stopped.

"They really don't like you, do they?" Daniel said as the door cracked in several places.

"I've had a few dealings with them," Alex tossed a sofa over and some other furniture to block the door.

"Actually we should be getting off this thing not blocking ourselves in. They may be about to blow it up," Daniel said as another piece of furniture landed at the door.

"They know blowing it up won't kill me," Alex went over to the port window, it wasn't big enough to get out. "Maybe they just wanted to get the two of us together and didn't know the best way to do it."

Daniel looked at him stunned. He shook his head and looked out of the window.

"It seems the people that are running things are as dangerous as what we are dealing with."

"Undoubtedly. Though I can see their point. They don't know what we're capable of or what will happen when they put us together. Why not let us have our meeting at sea where there is less to damage if we don't get on, Menarty" Alex stepped away.

"Oh, hold on a sec," Daniel raised his hand involuntary to point at himself. "You can't believe that I'm this thing they're searching for?"

"It is a possibility," Alex said moving into a good defensive position.

"It could just as easily be you, except I know that it isn't. I can feel that. Don't you feel anything about me," the dog had padded over to Daniel and stood at his side. The golden eyes stared at Alex with an intensity that forced him to take a step backwards.

263

"There seems to be definitely something odd about your dog," Alex said.

"Yes, he is different, I can feel that. But he is not bad. He saved my life."

"Maybe he is Menarty's pet," Alex said but even as he said it, he knew it was untrue.

"They told you to kill me?" Daniel looked wounded. "I've done my best to help them, to prove myself." He sat down on the bed and the dog rested its head in his lap.

Alex walked over to him. "I don't believe you are Menarty." He said.

"For all we know they already found this man and infected him, he might be the one giving the orders." He held his hand out to Daniel who stood and shook it. A warm smile of relief flooded his face.

"Don't look so relieved," Alex said. "We are still stuck on a zombie ship which is about to get blown up and the people out there are no friendlier."

"What do you suggest," Daniel said, he suddenly felt old and tired. The dog put a large paw in this lap and he stroked it's head.

"We could just wait for them to blow it up. I know it won't kill me and I'm assuming you have the same regenerative power?"

"The dog wouldn't survive." Daniel said and stood up. He paced to the portal and suddenly punched through it. The glass shattered and the zombies stared groaning and banging on the door again.

"Okay," Alex said. He moved to the other side of the portal, they both took hold around the shattered edge and then pulled in opposite directions, ripping the wall away until it was big enough for them to jump into the water.

"Where do we swim to? Daniel asked.

"I think we go deep, far enough away that they think we are down with the ship. Then we return to New York and seek out some allies."

They were still discussing it when the ship blew up. Daniel felt himself flying up into the air, his body seem to be hurting everywhere. Then everything went black and he felt himself sinking into the depth of the sea surrounded by dead bodies still moving and arms that seemed to try to swim on their own to some imagined body that was still in one piece. Daniel tried to move his arms to swim upward and then discovered the right side of his body was almost completely gone. He thought he saw the dog swimming towards him, bathed in a golden light, it's fur shining surrounded by a bubble that seemed to protect it.

Daniel's eyes closed and his last thought was regret, more than that it was the feeling of someone who had just found their destiny and then had lost it forever, desolation and grief descended on him as he continued to sink to the bottom of the ocean.

Alex had been blown the other way, he couldn't see where Daniel had gone in the darkness of the water but he searched for him and hoped that he was still alive. He wasn't sure what he would find, he had seen fragments of Daniel blow past him as the blast hit. Alex had remained intact, his body was anticipating every injury and repaired itself on impact. It felt tingly but no pain, the dog had disappeared. Alex was sure that at the moment of impact the dog just vanished. Then he had caught sight of it swimming down into the depths, a strange glow around it's body.

Alex followed, his body found a way to expel the water and pull the oxygen from the water. He continued until it was so dark that he lost sight of the golden glow of the dog, it was moving so fast. He stopped and was then spun around and around by a giant underwater wave. When he stopped spinning he couldn't tell if he was upside down or which way was back to the surface. He supposed he should thank the scientists for trying to kill him so many ways that he was protected from them but how would his body react to the pressure if he swam the wrong way and ended up on the bottom of the sea.

All at once, through the darkness below him he saw the golden glow getting nearer. It was heading straight for him and the remaining attached arm of Daniel in its mouth. There didn't seem to be enough of him left for him to be alive. The dog swam past him slowly and looked at him, he took hold of its mane, then the dog swam faster, onward and upward until the light could be seen through the water. As they went up, debris and zombies were still going down but the golden shield around the dog now encompassed all of them. As they neared the top the dog veered off to the side of where the ship had been, Alex could see something glittering in front of them, then they passed through it and they were on a dry surface. It felt warm underneath and it was light, Alex looked over at Daniel and felt a pang of loss. He had only known him for a short while and yet it felt like losing a brother.

He sat up and looked at the dog, he half expected it to speak but it just gazed back at him with soulful eyes.

"So this is your spaceship" Alex said at last.

The dog looked over and then lay down beside Daniel or what was left of him

"Well, grateful as I am that you showed me the way. I need to get back on real ground and find out who is to blame for this."

"It is the fear of man," the voice seem to be in Alex's head. He looked around and his eyes came back to rest on the dog. Yes it was the dog, he thought, it is in my head.

"My form is not built for speaking," the voice continued, "but if you prefer I could bark at the same time as you hear the words?"

"No, that's fine. You don't need to bark, you just carry on what you are doing and fill me in as to who you are and why you dragged him up here." Alex gestured at Daniel but as he did so he froze and then smiled. Daniel's body was regenerating and at a very fast rate. Already his right side had reappeared and his head wound was gone.

"He's alive?" Alex asked.

The dog nodded and walked over to the wall which then became a window, one way Alex presumed. They could see the desolation left behind and now navy vehicles were combing the area.

"We are a friendly race," the dog said. " We watch other civilisations normally in the form of pets they like. This is very similar to how we look at home. We never interfere in what is happening with a planet, apart from today when I saved this one's life." The dog walked around Daniel and nudged him. Daniel moved and started to groan.

"Can you help us," Alex asked.

"We cannot interfere with this planet's destiny. We are supposed to just watch, not participate."

"But you did, you saved him. Why did you do that?"

The dog looked pensive, as if he should not be giving anything away. "Because only he can defeat Menarty," he said suddenly.

Alex felt an unexpected pang of disappointment.

"I thought that I was the only one that could defeat Menarty?"

The dog moved over to him and looked deep into his eyes.

"You will do it together. But you can't do it without him."

"Should I ask why?" Alex stroked the dog without thinking, then withdrew his hand.

"It's okay, I like that," the dog sat down and shook his head. "Danny has something special about him."

"I gather we both do," Alex said as he glanced at Daniel to see that he was completely healed.

"Regeneration is not the gift you need to defeat Menarty. It is something far rarer."

The dog stood up and closed his eyes, the ship started to move away from the debris and army boats and picked up speed.

"I will leave you both on land and you must make your way to Washington. Speak with the president, he will give you the back-up you need to set up a real team. Before you can get to Menarty you must go through his trusted minions, they must not be allowed build his army."

Alex was about to ask about Caroline and Samantha, to ask what it was all about when the dog suddenly barked.

"Don't ask me to intercede anymore, I have already done more than I should. To get to the president you need to go into the bunker beneath the white house, the code is 4372578. You get to it by entering the lobby, going straight ahead to a large painting and then clicking the painting to the side. You can figure the rest out."

The ship stopped and Alex saw that they were by land.

"My ship is only invisible when landed, it does not fly without being seen."

"That's not very advanced" Alex said as he helped a dazed Daniel to his feet.

The dog seemed to chortle. "Advanced enough.

"One more thing," Alex waited for the dog to make eye contact. "Can we give others the power of.....invincibility, so that they can't be killed?"

The dog gave an involuntary whimper. "Many will die, they cannot be changed or saved. At the end there will be more than one life force inhabiting the Earth and you will need to learn to live together or destroy everything.

Besides, you already know that you can be killed. My mate told you that, there are strange things at work here, powers that can harm you."

'So, you could sense I met your friend?'

'Yes, I can still smell her on you. I know she is alive, if anything happened to her, I would be aware.'

A door opened and the dog looked away so Alex helped Daniel onto the land. He was already starting to wake up.

"Wait!" The dogs voice seemed to scream in Alex's head.

The dog trotted over to Daniel, he had just woken and looked in the dog's eye and then hugged him.

"So glad you made it boy, I was worried about you." He ruffled the dog's fur and then the dog moved back into the ship. "Goodbye," Alex heard the dog say.

"Where are you going? What is this?" Daniel watched as the space ship's door closed and the dog vanished, he turned to Alex. "What's going on now?"

"Could you hear the dog say goodbye?" Alex asked.

"Hear him?" Daniel repeated. "As in speaking?"

Alex couldn't help feeling a bit smug. He could talk to the animals, at least one of them. "I'll fill you in as we make our way to Washington."

"I've been there already, I don't think they will be of any help," Daniel said.

"Well the dog seemed to think the president would help." Alex said quietly

Daniel sensed that Alex felt he was two steps ahead. "His spaceship did seem similar to the other one," Daniel said.

"The other one?" Alex asked.

"Yes, it seems you don't know everything, Alex Cartier."

Alex fell silent and thought about Samantha, he would have given anything to know where she was now and whether she was safe. He just hoped that Frank really would protect her.

Epilogue

Frank walked forward to the waiting group, he held Samantha's hand and took her with him. She tried to pull him back but he looked at her with a new presence, his eyes not black, his fingernails not long. That same smile on his lips that she remembered from before he became a hardened government agent and he looked younger, alive and strong. His head was no longer bald and patchy, his hair now thick and dark. He squeezed her hand and took her forward.

"I am Menarty," he said to the waiting crowds.

Published by Brave New World International Ltd.

United Kingdom. Tel +44 0207 118 6249

23011074R00157

Printed in Poland
by Amazon Fulfillment
Poland Sp. z o.o., Wrocław